glee
SUMMER BREAK

Also Available

Hachette Book Group ★ 237 Park Avenue, New York, NY 10017 ★ For more of your favorite series, visit our website at www.pickapoppy.com ★ Poppy is an imprint of Little, Brown and Company. The Poppy name and logo are trademarks of Hachette Book Group, Inc.

The publisher is not responsible for websites (or their content) that are not owned by the publisher.

First Edition: July 2011

ISBN 978-0-316-12360-0

10 9 8 7 6 5 4 3 2 1 ★ RRD-C ★ Printed in the United States of America

glee

SUMMER BREAK

AN ORIGINAL NOVEL

BY SOPHIA LOWELL

BASED ON THE SERIES CREATED BY
RYAN MURPHY & BRAD FALCHUK & IAN BRENNAN

poppy

LITTLE, BROWN AND COMPANY
NEW YORK ★ BOSTON

one

Rachel Berry's bedroom, Monday morning

A tiny drop of sweat inched its way down Rachel Berry's cheekbone and rolled delicately onto her pink floral pillowcase. Sunshine was surging through her curtains, illuminating her just as a strong spotlight should. It was as if her room were a Broadway stage and the light had finally found its star. Rachel stirred, rubbing her eyes and sleepily stretching herself awake. A smile spread across her face. Sunshine like that could mean only one thing: Beautiful, delicious summer was about to be here. And it was all hers!

The *Wicked* calendar on her wall, with its neatly drawn x's inked with a chartreuse glitter pen on each day, signaled that there was only one more week left at McKinley High School. One more *measly* little week before

Rachel's time completely belonged to her. Five days, that was it.

"Good morning, Patti!" she said to her brand-new ceramic bust of Broadway legend Patti LuPone. It was an early end-of-year gift from her dads. They'd even wrapped it in *Sweeney Todd* wrapping paper. You really could buy anything online these days.

Rachel began humming a pitch-perfect rendition of "Oh, What a Beautiful Mornin'" from *Oklahoma!* as she booted up her computer. *I got a beautiful feelin', everything's goin' my way.* The lyrics seemed fitting, but she sang them only inside her head. One's vocal cords needed time to wake up. Not worth risking an injury.

As she typed her password, Rachel wondered if this feeling of impending freedom could ever be matched by anything other than the end of a school year. Probably not. Maybe the end of a yearlong run as Maria in *West Side Story*, but even *that* would be bittersweet. When that day came (and it would), she would be showered with praise and admiration — which is more than she could say currently of her Glee Club counterparts. They were all way too self-involved with their silly issues to congratulate her daily on her numerous talents.

But that didn't matter for now — it was going to be Rachel's summer. Or, as the brightly colored Excel spreadsheet now open on her desktop proclaimed, RACHEL'S STAR POWER SUMMER! It was going to be a tightly packed, intensive schedule consisting of various classes, training sessions, and even an impossible-to-secure meeting with a real Broadway talent agency. Rachel had charted her very own way to the stars. She was like Galileo, only tinier and with much more charisma.

Rachel assessed the schedule once more. She was positively brimming with excitement at the strides she was going to make in her career from the rigorous workload. Of course, it didn't seem like work to her. She was a girl who made things happen for herself — and sometimes for her fellow Glee Club members. Not that they had a choice once Rachel decided to include them in her agenda. Resistance was futile.

This time, the lucky recipient of her wishes was none other than Finn Hudson — the leading man who somehow always maintained a notable presence in her life, whether they were together or not. They'd reconnected and broken up so many times that no one at McKinley High could even keep track of their status anymore. They'd come to accept that Finn and Rachel would always be drifting in and out of each other's orbits. It was just a question of whether the planets were aligned that day.

Rachel tore her eyes away from her schedule for just a moment to cast a dreamy glance at the glittery picture frame on her desk. It contained a snapshot of her and Finn gazing into each other's eyes, taken while singing the Journey medley onstage at last year's regionals. A great shot.

She was proud of him — she really was. Finn had come so far in Glee Club. She appreciated the improvement more than anyone else. But Rachel always saw new ways to sculpt people into perfect specimens. Finn was no exception. His dancing skills were atrocious. One time last year, when they were rehearsing for regionals, Finn had crissed when he should have crossed. He accidentally smacked both Rachel and Quinn Fabray in the face. Not that Rachel minded so much about Quinn (actually she really enjoyed it), but Rachel's face was very precious. It was going to be the second reason she was famous. Her voice would be the first.

Lots of the kids in Glee could use practice in dancing, but Finn needed it most. So Rachel had taken it upon herself to include him in her Star Power Summer. Not that he knew it yet. She had seen an ad for couples ballroom-dancing classes in the back of an issue of *Ohio Bride* magazine (which she flipped through at the bookstore sometimes to look at the gorgeous ball gowns). Obviously, she wasn't gearing up to marry Finn or anything. This was just the perfect venue for them to practice some much-needed partnering skills. Besides, Rachel thought it seemed incredibly romantic.

Rachel imagined that twice a week at the dance studio a scene would unfold just like the one in *Singin' in the Rain* where Don Lockwood and Kathy Selden waltzed through the empty soundstage. Rachel would float in wearing a gauzy dress, her dark hair fashioned into a finger wave. Then she would be swept into the debonair arms of a suit-and-tie-wearing gentleman. If all went according to plan, it was going to be perfect. She couldn't wait to tell Finn when she got to school.

A lemon-yellow sundress and red sequined ballet flats sat

expectantly on the cushy armchair by her bed. Her outfit for the day was perfectly suited to match her sunny mood. Rachel believed that success was the result of preparation-meets-opportunity—she could never be too prepared in any aspect of her life, including each day at McKinley. That was why she always finished her homework before singing an entire Broadway soundtrack each evening. And that was also why it was absolutely essential to choose each outfit the night before.

As Rachel began getting dressed, she went over her new summer schedule in her head. Mondays would start each week off with a four-hour studio session at Lima's only recording studio, Lima Beats. It wasn't much—just an old converted house downtown that some ex–record producer named Tito opened up a few years back. Its customers mainly consisted of pimpled teenage boys in garage bands with MySpace pages and ridiculous names like Twisted Agony. All very amateur stuff. Of course, that would all change when Rachel stepped through the door and began recording her album of Idina Menzel cover songs. Rachel's voice was going to sound even more amazing on professional recording equipment. She just knew it. No Auto-Tune necessary.

Tuesdays and Thursdays would begin with tap, jazz, and ballet classes, followed by elocution lessons with a local private tutor, Sir Paul Stanton. He was a friend of her dads' and had apparently attended Oxford University and everything. He had already assigned her a book to read before her first lesson—*Elements of Elocution*, by some old-timey actor named John Walker. It did sound a bit dry, if Rachel was being honest with herself. But she personally thought that proper pronunciation was an oft-overlooked yet very important skill for any performer to possess. She had pointed this fact out to her fellow Glee member Tina Cohen-Chang once during practice last year and had received little thanks for her efforts.

Tina had been trying to suggest a new song for the club to practice, but every title that had passed through her lips had been peppered with stutters. Rachel thought it sounded worse than when someone's nails accidentally scratched the chalkboard in math class. Or when Noah "Puck" Puckerman did it on purpose just to watch everyone cringe. After Tina suggested doing a song by the "B-B-B-Buh-Beach Boys," Rachel could stand it no longer and lectured the group on the importance of speech lessons. Tina ran out of the choir room crying, and once again Rachel was greeted by nothing but angry expressions and crossed arms. Except from Brittany Pierce, of course, who had asked if she could bring her cat to the speech lessons. Apparently, poor Britt had been having trouble understanding the kitty over all the extremely loud purring.

Rachel was used to being chided for her efforts, though. Just because others didn't care whether they sounded like uneducated country bumpkins didn't mean she couldn't. She had clocked enough hours watching *My Fair Lady* to learn that lesson! Anyway, it turned out that Tina had only been faking the awful stutter. Why someone would want to make herself sound anything less than perfectly poised was absolutely unfathomable to Rachel.

As she brushed her shiny dark locks and stared at her reflection, Rachel's smirk faded to a frown as she noticed the beginnings of a tan line on her shoulders. It must have been from the camisole she had worn in the backyard. She had spent some time out there over the weekend memorizing a new monologue from *In the Heights*.

Rachel had to be careful in the sun. Her skin browned very easily. Unlike the Cheerios—who were practically tanorexic with their Sue Sylvester–funded addiction to the sun beds down at Total Tan—Rachel didn't like to over-expose herself. She wanted her skin to remain young and beautiful forever. She would never understand Coach Sylvester's obsession with the look of a fake tan against a Cheerios uniform. Regardless, a visible tan line was *so* not part of Rachel's plan, especially because she had just booked a photographer to take her head shots this Saturday.

She needed something that looked extremely professional yet screamed "future star" to hand to the casting directors at her upcoming auditions. The head shots would also come in handy for signing autographs for her adoring fans. She was going to give one to Breadstix to hang on the wall, where people could admire Rachel's megawatt smile and ponder her humble beginnings while they ate their spaghetti and meatballs. She would sign it, "To Breadstix, Thanks for all the pasta and good times! Ciao! Rachel Berry." It was a far cry from Sardi's in New York City, but it would have to do. The restaurant would certainly thank her for it later, when her photo drew in lots of business.

Rachel reminded herself to call the photographer to confirm her appointment. She also had to e-mail some outfit options to him. She was thinking polka dots, but did they seem like too bold a choice? Quickly typing a note into her spreadsheet, she double-checked the rest of her smorgasbord of training sessions. Voice? *Check.* Acting? *Check.* Ballroom dancing with a hunky male lead? *Check, please!* She printed out three copies of her schedule and scribbled *Rachel Berry* in the top-left corner of one, then *Finn* and *Mr. Schuester* on the other two. The one that bore her name was marked with a gold star sticker, of course. At this point, it was still just a metaphor for stardom. But soon it would be true!

She thought it was important to keep Mr. Schuester in the loop on all her plans. He should know how dedicated she was to continuing her training throughout the summer and be able to refer to the schedule at any moment during vacation in case he needed to contact her about set lists for next year.

Since Mr. Schuester's Glee takeover, Rachel had been carrying the majority of the club's vocal weight. She had suspected this on several occasions and even proved it once by bribing Lauren Zizes from the AV Club to secretly tape the other kids during practice. Hardly *any* of them had been singing at all! Being the most talented, she didn't mind much. But if she was going to be the one doing all the heavy lifting, she should have certain power when it came to song selections and costume ideas. That was why she always took every opportunity to make her opinions known, much to the chagrin of her lazy New Directions teammates. And man, were they lazy.

Rachel grabbed her brand-new copy of the McKinley High *Thunderclap* from the top of her white lacquered dresser. It was so heavy, almost like a textbook. The shiny black cover was emblazoned with the school's red-and-white crest. The symbol seemed to give Rachel that giddy feeling of anticipation she got when she watched the opening credits of *The Music Man* and knew she was about to experience a musical tour de force on-screen.

Despite the substantial weight, it was the one book that students from any clique at school didn't mind carrying around. Yearbooks had always been kind of a big deal at McKinley High. And they were sort of a game for Rachel. She liked to make sure her presence at the school was known by appearing in as many pictures as possible. It would prepare her for the days when her face would grace the covers of fashion and star magazines. Sadly, she had little control over her appearances in the yearbook. Most of the photo spreads were of the Cheerios doing backflips and flirting with the football team between classes. However, the one trump card she did hold was her secret weapon, Jacob Ben Israel. To Rachel, "J-Fro" was extremely creepy, almost like a stalker at times, but he was also a *Thunderclap* photographer. And that meant she had to play up the charm around him a bit every year during layout finalization. It was great acting practice.

This year, she had let J-Fro include her in a feature called "A Day in the Life," which followed different McKinley students around during the same day at school. Rachel was ecstatic to be selected—the feature would probably have double the number of pictures of her that appeared in the previous year's edition. She even allowed J-Fro to begin the day at her house, taking pictures of her getting ready in her bedroom while she sang her morning scales ("*me me me me me me me me meeee*"). He scampered around all day behind her like a clumsy, drooling puppy with a frizzy Afro, snapping away and asking her incredibly invasive questions.

She fired off answers like a true professional. It was only when J-Fro got to "What color underwear do you have on today?" that Rachel gave the most celebrity-like answer of them all: "No comment." She doubted that part would appear in the *Thunderclap*, but she had been in the moment.

Rachel flipped to the feature she had so eagerly awaited all semester. She had held off until she was home to give it her full attention and properly soak up each detail. It hadn't come out quite how she'd expected it to.

It looked more like the back section of *Us Weekly* where the magazine picked apart fashions and made jokes than a young starlet's profile in *Vogue*. Not one of the photos was flattering. There she was, singing in her bedroom with morning hair sticking out in every direction. Getting slushied in the hallway. An action shot of her singing and dancing in Glee Club, giving it her all while the others around her either looked bored or rolled their eyes. *Well, at least it's accu-*

rate, she thought. And even if it didn't paint her in the best light, it was Rachel's first two-page spread. Her dads had been proud. They reminded her of the showbiz adage "Bad publicity is better than no publicity at all." At least people at school were talking about her.

When the yearbooks were handed out yesterday, J-Fro had practically groveled at Rachel's feet for forgiveness. It didn't shock her. It seemed like he was always begging Rachel for something. He claimed that some of the Cheerios had sabotaged his original layout as a prank — they had stolen his camera and used the rejected photos of her that he was keeping for "personal use." By the time he'd found out, the proofs had already been sent to the printer and were being prepped for binding. When she'd asked him what he meant by "personal use," J-Fro darted out of the room, wailing something about how the photos couldn't legally be taken away from him.

Part of being unstoppable was being resilient. Rachel was able to let this little publicity hiccup roll right off her back. In addition to witnessing the annual McKinley High tradition of defacing the Glee Club group photo in the *Thunderclap*, Rachel was used to virtual taunting. Snide comments on her YouTube videos were a daily occurrence, so it was a good thing Rachel had developed a thick skin.

For example, she had recently received a comment on her a cappella rendition of Eminem and Rihanna's "Love the Way You Lie" from a user named WMHS_CheerioBrittz. It said, *You should stay inside the computer screen, all tiny and stuff. It's cuter and way less annoying than you normally are.*

BTW, how did you get in there...? Even Brittany, who sometimes seemed as if she had an IQ lower than her age, had managed to insult her. Not *well*, but still. Rachel knew what it was like to be constantly berated and underappreciated by the popular kids.

But surprisingly, those other Glee kids could be the worst of them all! With the constant bickering and social drama that went on within the four walls of their inadequate choir room, sometimes it seemed more like an episode of *Jersey Shore* than a professional music group. Just last week, Mercedes Jones and Santana Lopez had gotten into another one of their heated diva-offs over who should get the Hayley Williams solo in a mash-up of B.o.B's "Airplanes" and John Denver's "Leaving on a Jet Plane." It was completely absurd. Mr. Schuester spent half of practice trying to mediate the fight, while everyone else just slacked off. Artie Abrams even fell asleep. Puck took the golden opportunity to draw some unsavory doodles all over Artie's face with a permanent marker. It was like working with children. Honestly.

But at least Rachel didn't have to worry about babysitting her classmates for the next three months. All she had to think about was number one—herself. Tucking the three schedules into the pages of her yearbook, Rachel blew herself a kiss in the mirror and bounded downstairs. She still had enough time to give her dads hugs and grab breakfast on her way out the door.

Rachel opened the freezer door and started searching for ingredients.

Breakfast was important. She liked to create her own unique juices and smoothies each morning to fend off any bugs she may have picked up in that disgusting petri dish of a school. All one had to do to catch a virus at McKinley was step through the door. Rachel always took necessary precautions. There was no way she was going to have an encore of her experience with laryngitis. Losing her voice had been traumatic, to say the least.

I love a good theme, Rachel thought as she tossed some fresh acai berries into her chrome ten-speed blender. She called it the StarBerry smoothie. It also required a scoop of ground flaxseeds, some raspberries, and sliced star fruit. A dash of pomegranate juice and crushed ice finished it off. She hit the BLEND option, and the sweet concoction whirled around, mixing together to create something delicious and unstoppable — not entirely unlike when all the members of New Directions actually played their parts, working together to create smooth melodies.

Rachel was totally the juice in that scenario, though. Without juice, things would get clogged in the blades, resulting in a lumpy mess. Glee Club needed Rachel like a smoothie needed juice. Yep, that was her, all right. Good old juice.

Too bad she didn't need the Glee kids. This summer, she was going to create her own sweet sounds. No matter what they had to say about it.

two

McKinley High entrance, Monday morning

A contented Mercedes Jones sat on the front steps of McKinley High, relishing the warmth of the morning sunshine on her face. The last week of school usually felt like a breeze. But this year was different. She still had a few big assignments hanging over her head, so she couldn't truly relax.

The most daunting was a final exam in Mr. Schuester's Spanish II class. Foreign languages were so not her strong point. Brushing the negative thoughts aside, she breathed in the fresh air and got lost in a daydream of lying by her cousin's pool. Ideally, she would be sporting her new zebra-striped Wayfarer sunglasses while flipping through *Superstar Weekly* and have absolutely, positively, *zero* Spanish homework. *Nada*.

But the impending Spanish doom wasn't the only thing that was bothering Mercedes. There was a tiny something else nagging her in the back of her mind. And it had to do with Glee Club. Or the lack of it.

For Mercedes, summer was always a time of goofing off. It consisted mainly of a combination of standing in long lines at the Lima Freeze to get Oreo milk shakes with Kurt Hummel, beating the heat in the cool air-conditioning at the mall, or even just chilling in her room, listening to new music she downloaded off iTunes. For a few months, Mercedes didn't have to worry about homework, grades, or surviving a day at McKinley High without getting slushied by her classmates. During the summer, the only slushies she would see were ones she bought for herself at the mini-mart. To *drink*. To be honest, though, she hadn't really had a taste for them the past few years. You could only get so much cherry-flavored ice in your face before you associated the taste with bad feelings and an outfit change.

Mercedes scanned the parking lot for any signs of her best friend. Kurt was still nowhere in sight, so Mercedes popped in her neon-yellow earbuds and scrolled to the B.o.B section on her iPod. She might as well use the last few minutes before school started to hear the solo again. She selected "Airplanes," which was one of her favorite songs even if it was starting to get played out. Currently it was the twenty-seventh most played on her list. The song began, and Mercedes drummed to the beat on her binder. She knew that she had to win that solo over Santana, even if it meant another argument that took up the whole period. *"I could use a dream or a genie or a wish,"* the song pulsed in her ears.

Mercedes didn't want to just keep wishing. Although she had always loved singing, it wasn't until recently that Mercedes started taking the hobby a little more seriously. Maybe it was the influence of that nut job Rachel Berry — but for once in her life, Mercedes thought she might actually stand a chance at a career in the performing arts. And with senior year approaching fast, she needed to start making some decisions — or at the very least, keep her vocal chops up in the off-season. Man, Mercedes was going to miss that silly Glee Club.

Luckily, the school year had hours upon hours of practice built into Mercedes's busy lifestyle. Every day at school, she could count on warming up with New Directions and belting out some sweet tunes (that is, if Rachel could stop berating the rest of the club long enough for them all to actually get some verses in). Mr. Schuester did his part by trying to get them to perform as often as they could. And even on Sundays, Mercedes could count on clocking some time singing with her church choir. It was all very convenient. A total no-brainer. Until now.

It didn't occur to Mercedes that she might be losing momentum until a few weeks ago after practice. She normally tuned Rachel out, but on this particular day Rachel was giving Sam Evans one of her "lessons." Sam had been new to McKinley at the beginning of the year, but he was a quick learner and had acclimated faster than a fish to water.

He certainly didn't need much help. Yet Rachel still insisted on teaching him useless facts from time to time and pretending it was charity. Everyone knew she just relished the opportunity to boss some new blood around. Poor guy. He was too nice to ignore her.

"Sam, I think it's important that you continue your pursuit of vocal perfection," Rachel had proclaimed.

To which Sam had replied nonchalantly, "Uhh, sure. Sounds good."

"Excellent choice. I think you'll find that a career in show business is not easy, but you have shown some early potential. With a ton more practice, I think you could be sculpted into something adequate. Perhaps part of an ensemble. Leads like me are always looking for a great ensemble to back them up. Have you considered your options?" The fervor with which Rachel interrogated him would seem psychotic to anyone who didn't know her.

"Options? I dunno, I guess I will just be in New Directions again next year or something...." Sam wasn't really listening anymore. He was too busy ogling Quinn Fabray, who had bent down to pick up a tube of glitter lip gloss she had purposely dropped on the floor. Her Cheerios skirt was pretty short.

"You wouldn't want to let those shiny new vocal cords of yours go dormant over the summer, would you?" Rachel's voice had become all breathy and desperate. "That would do practically the same damage as shouting at the top of your lungs for a week straight! Did you know that if you don't use it, you really *do* lose it?" Thankfully, Mercedes hadn't heard the rest of the conversation, because Rachel followed Sam and Quinn out of the choir room and beyond.

Girl needs to learn to take a hint, Mercedes had thought. Maybe one of the AV kids could create an app on Rachel's cell phone that beeped when she became annoying. On the other hand, it would probably turn into one constant, eternal beep.

Even though what Rachel had said about losing your voice if you didn't use it was decidedly ridiculous, Mercedes secretly thought she did have the tiniest little bit of a point. This, quite frankly, scared Mercedes because Rachel didn't often make sense. It was fine for Sam or the other kids, who were only a part of Glee to make the school year more bearable, to slack off during summer. But maybe Mercedes should get a little more serious.

Her only chance to perform for a large crowd during the summer was at her church's annual Fourth of July barbecue. Every year, the church rented the outdoor stage at the Lima Community Park and put on a patriotic musical revue. People would come with their picnic baskets and blankets, staking out seats in the early morning and throughout the day. Mercedes would just chill with her family and eat tons of tasty food, including her mom's famous potato salad. That dish even eclipsed the deliciousness of McKinley High Tater Tots.

Then, when dusk fell and the crowd had fallen into a happy, satiated post-food haze, the show would begin. The costumes weren't much — just T-shirts in red, white, or blue and sequined top hats that had been used for so long that most of the sequins were falling off. It was the closest to a packed auditorium she had ever gotten until nationals in New York this year. And for the past two years, Mercedes had been selected by her peers to sing "The Star-Spangled Banner" during the meager fireworks display. It was pretty nice to be recognized as the star of the group, unlike at school, where it seemed that Rachel had claimed that title for all of time. Rumors had been circulating among the congregation that Mercedes was going to be chosen for a record-breaking third year. Fourth of July was her favorite day of the summer. A guaranteed good time, filled with music and friends.

But as much as she loved performing with her church choir, it lacked in certain departments, which Glee usually made up for. For example, the only dance moves the choir ever did had to match the abilities of a seventy-year-old grandmother. It wasn't really Mrs. Wilkins's fault, though. Mercedes didn't mind including everyone (it *was* church, after all), but she had come to really enjoy the challenge of matching her melodies to elaborate, choreographed routines. She knew she had some serious moves. Why shouldn't she get to show them off?

Mercedes knew hip-hop better than anyone at McKinley High. Mike Chang argued that *he* did, but homeboy was seriously kidding himself. Sure, he was good, but he lacked a certain something. Last year, when she and Kurt had done a brief stint on the Cheerios, all the red-and-black-clad McKinley robots had managed to loosen up a little under her supervision. She even made them look a little human. Mercedes could only imagine how great the squad might be if they employed more funky moves regularly. Didn't those girls learn anything from *Bring It On?* Mercedes secretly loved that movie, even if it was about cheerleaders. Maybe it was because the squad of stiff automatons in red uniforms got schooled by the soulful, inner-city girls with the hip-hop-infused routine. It showed that you shouldn't mess with the power of funk, which was a valuable lesson indeed.

Mercedes quickly typed a note to herself into her phone to slip a copy of the DVD through the slots in Brittany's locker, Netflix-style. At the very least, it would be entertaining to watch Brittany try to figure that one out. She would probably think it was an offering from the "Spirit Gods," like she did that time when she found a pair of her old Cheerios briefs under the bleachers during litter detention. Mercedes was pretty sure Brittany had just left them there during a completely inappropriate make-out session with that kid from the tennis team, Charlie Reeves. Brittany, however, insisted they were delivered back to her by a pelican. "He's their messenger bird," she'd explained. Mercedes thought that girl had fallen off of one too many human pyramids.

Mercedes minimized the note application and practically jumped when she saw the time. *8:13!* The bell should have rung three minutes ago! Sure enough, when she looked up, it was like a ghost town. She must have had the volume of the music up too high. Damn. The only students left were a few latecomers scrambling up the steps, juggling books and boxes of orange juice while rubbing sleep out of their eyes. But still no Kurt Hummel.

Mercedes should have been worried about being late to class, but this was very weird. Kurt was almost never late. In fact, she could only remember two mornings in the past few years when he hadn't been at least ten minutes early. "Early bird gets the best worms, and the best off-the-rack Dolce and Gabbana," he'd always remind her. The first time he'd been late had been because of his inability to accept Lady Gaga's decision to start wearing pants. He'd stayed up really late the night before Photoshopping a campaign poster that displayed "the repercussions of a style icon bending to the petty whims of polite society." It had a picture of a tiger wearing pants and the slogan TIGERS DON'T WEAR PANTS. NEITHER SHOULD GAGA. He'd hoped it would go viral. It didn't. Good thing Lady Gaga still sported jeweled panties occasionally on her way to the airport.

The only other instance Kurt had been late was during the Dave Karofsky bullying incident, when he was too afraid to come to school. Mercedes sincerely hoped this time was nothing like that. Especially since Kurt had finally rejoined New Directions and McKinley High after a hiatus spent at Dalton Academy. Mercedes was pretty sure everything was fine. But she should probably wait for him, just in case. With any luck, he had just decided to stop at that new bakery next to LaPaloma's to get the two of them some fresh cinnamon buns for breakfast. Mercedes's mouth started watering like

Pavlov's dog at the delicious prospect. Class could definitely wait.

It was almost ten minutes after the first bell when Kurt's black SUV finally screeched to a halt into one of the unshaded spots in the McKinley parking lot. Both students and teachers avoided these undesirable sunny spots at the end of the school year because the pavement got so hot, you could fry an egg on it. Some of the guys from the football team had even tried to do that once instead of egging Finn Hudson's car, as they had originally intended to. Mercedes thought it was funny how easily amused those oafs were sometimes. Such simple minds, such simple pleasures.

A frazzled-looking Kurt tumbled out of his car unceremoniously. He grabbed his distressed-leather satchel and fumbled for his keys. He double-clicked the button as he ran up the steps to meet Mercedes. The loud honk signaled his car was locked, but it also made their presence known to Principal Figgins, who was across the lot, sipping his morning coffee. It was most likely a latte from Coach Sylvester, who liked to butter him up with unsolicited treats every time she was about to make a ridiculous request on behalf of her Cheerios. Which was often.

"Where in the Mariah Carey have you been?" Mercedes stage-whispered as she began to take in Kurt's unkempt appearance. She could see Figgins making his way toward them with a furrowed brow. The entire student body at McKinley knew that Principal Figgins's main rules were "no monkeyshines, no sass-back, and no lollygagging." Mercedes still wasn't sure what the first one even meant, but she didn't want to get caught doing the other two. Mercedes often provided sass-back, and right now they were most definitely lollygagging and late for class.

"Hurry up! I sure as hell ain't spending *my* last week in litter detention!" She grabbed Kurt by the arm and pulled him inside.

"Go ahead. My shirt is already wrinkled," Kurt announced dramatically. "And I have worn this outfit before. So it doesn't even matter...." He tried to smooth down a piece of hair that was pointed skyward. "I'm such a failure."

Mercedes took stock. He was wearing a pair of blue-and-white seersucker shorts with a brown leather belt, a crisp white button-down, and a red-striped bow tie. It looked pretty standard Kurt to her. Mercedes considered herself a fashionista, but he somehow always managed to cling to tiny details that no one else would ever notice. She had learned that lesson earlier this year after wearing the same rhinestone pendant of a boom box three days in a row. Kurt had been less than subtle when he asked her if she needed him to go accessories shopping with her after school. Sometimes he was best taken with a grain of salt. This was one of those times.

"Have you been inhaling too many fumes at your dad's tire shop? What I wanna know is, why are you so late? Please tell me nothing is wrong and that you brought me the Spanish notes from last week." Mercedes's face twisted into the expression of a puppy dog awaiting a Milk-Bone. Kurt's attention to detail certainly paid off when it came to his class notes, which she sometimes borrowed. And Mercedes could use all the help she could get right about now.

"Ugh, I can't even *think* about homework at a time like this." Kurt shuddered. "My life is over."

"Did Katy Perry decide to stop wearing bras in the shape of cupcakes or something?" Mercedes retorted, wishing she had just gone to art class. Ms. Kowalski never took attendance anyway, and Mercedes wasn't sure she wanted to deal with Kurt's issues on top of her own (especially without the Spanish notes she'd been promised). "If you are going to be such a drama queen, you can at least clue me in." She followed Kurt to his locker.

"I am doomed to a summer of outfit repeats. My dad"— Kurt sighed heavily before gathering the strength to continue—"took away my clothing allowance and eBay privileges. It's a cruel and unusual punishment for such a minor offense!" He rummaged through his locker like a maniac, even accidentally ripping the corner of the picture of his friend Blaine from Dalton Academy. "I thought I had a—aha!" Kurt produced a white bow tie and a white canvas belt and proceeded to quick-change with the alacrity of a Broadway professional right there in the humble halls of McKinley.

"What exactly did you do?" Mercedes's interest was slightly piqued. Kurt didn't get into trouble too often.

"Last night I got sucked into a *What Not to Wear* marathon while I was doing my homework. Carole came in and asked if she could do anything to help . . . and I told her that it would help *everyone* if she didn't wear pants from three seasons ago," Kurt recounted.

Mercedes jaw dropped. "You told your new stepmother what?"

"I didn't mean it! You *know* how I tend to absorb the persona of characters if I watch them for too long. Especially Stacy and Clinton." Mercedes nodded knowingly, recalling the time Kurt had gotten sucked into an *America's Next Top Model* marathon. He had watched almost three cycles before morphing into a weird version of Tyra Banks. He kept coaching everyone on how to "smile with your eyes," or, as he kept saying, "smizing."

Kurt continued. "Anyway, my dad overheard it. He thinks I am becoming too superficial and selfish. I spent all morning trying to convince him otherwise. But he still says he won't give me back my allowance until I prove that I am doing something to help others. And it can't even be a makeover on some girl . . . or me." Kurt's shoulders slumped in defeat.

Burt Hummel sure knows his baby well, Mercedes thought. The boy loved makeovers a little too much.

"Any suggestions?" he whined, straightening the fresh bow tie in the reflection of his locker mirror. The frame was emblazoned with scrolled letters that asked WHO'S THE FAIR-EST? It was an obvious throwback to Snow White, which made Mercedes chuckle. Much like the original asker of the question, Kurt could certainly be the biggest drama queen. She wondered if the mirror's message was intentional.

Mercedes wrapped up her earbuds, which had gotten mad-tangled in the dash from Figgins. She finally offered, "Well, once a month I go with my mom and some friends from church to visit the elderly at the retirement home. I can ask if you can come. We play games and stuff."

Kurt wrinkled his nose. "Thanks, but no thanks. Ever since competing against that old Hipsters group at sectionals, I haven't been able to get the smell of Geritol out of my nose."

Mercedes thought that was a little extreme. She'd thought that the Hipsters were sort of charming, but maybe it was because she was used to performing with Mrs. Wilkins. Kurt clearly had a long way to go in the whole selflessness department.

Come to think of it, he hadn't even asked how she was doing. Nor did he seem to care that they were both extremely tardy. He slammed his locker shut, popped a piece of peppermint gum in his mouth, and whipped out his cell.

"Any chance I can have a package shipped to your house? I just bid on a vintage straw fedora that was *made* for my beachwear, and I can't let my dad see it." He was now tapping furiously on the screen. Kurt was somehow one of the only kids in school who managed to get around the McKinley High official no-cell-phone-during-school-hours policy.

At that precise moment, Mercedes's ears perked up to a familiar sound. The purposeful squeak of athletic shoes on the shiny linoleum unmistakably belonged to Coach Sue Sylvester and her less imposing lackeys Santana Lopez and

Brittany Pierce. Today, Coach Sylvester was sporting a navy blue tracksuit with red and white stripes.

Upon spotting the two renegades, Coach Sylvester immediately pivoted on her heel and changed course. She never missed an opportunity to belittle an underling.

"I'm not nearly as concerned about your blatant disregard for punctuality as I am about your obvious intention to injure my eyes by wearing that hideous outfit. At least now I know why they call it seer*sucker*. That's right, because you, my friend, are a sucker. Get to class, Porcelain. You, too, Queen Latifah," Coach Sylvester barked before powering down the corridor.

"B-T-dubs, Colonel Sanders, changing the bow tie does *not* make it a new outfit," Santana added, and sashayed off after Coach Sylvester.

Before falling in line, Brittany regarded him with a cocked head and her usual gentle, childlike voice. "Whenever people wear all white, I think they sometimes look like toilets. Is that why she called you Porcelain?"

Kurt shook his head dejectedly. He gave Brittany a condescending pat on the top of her blond high ponytail before she scampered off to follow her leader.

"Well, girl's got that right. People *do* give you a lot of crap," said Mercedes, cracking a smile.

"True. But they actually had a point!" Kurt insisted. He took Mercedes's hands and begged. "I look awful. You have to help me find a way to fix this. I refuse to ruin my impeccable wardrobe record over something so silly." He flicked his man-bangs out of the way.

Mercedes rolled her eyes. He really seemed to be entirely missing his dad's point. But maybe she could come up with something to make Kurt Hummel a more giving person.

"Fine. But you know what it'll cost ya...." she said as she finally started toward the art room. A squeal of delight took the place of Kurt's answer.

Mercedes had a feeling there would be a hot-from-the-oven cinnamon bun waiting with her name on it tomorrow morning. If only it came with a side of super-fresh summer plans. Now that would be the *real* icing on the cake.

three

Choir room, Monday afternoon

I t was generally understood that the last week of school at McKinley was not meant to be productive. It was hard enough getting the students, who usually had the attention spans of goldfish, to focus during the long school year without the added distraction of yearbooks and skin-baring summer outfits. Of course, a handful of the more strict teachers, like Mr. Hausler, took a stand against this lackadaisical attitude by scheduling their final exams for Monday or Tuesday of the last week. They did this purely to inflict their power one last time before they had none for three months. At least that was Artie Abrams's theory. Why else would they want to ruin everyone's fun? They clearly enjoyed torturing nervous juniors (such as themselves) who were getting ready to apply to colleges by forcing them to study extra hard when they should be having fun.

Mercedes wasn't the only one with the future on her mind. Most of the members of New Directions were starting to think about their post-McKinley plans. Summer had certainly crept up on them, and senior year was not far behind. The summer months always had a habit of speeding by faster than Kurt picking through clothes at a Prada sample sale. But at least there was a little more time to goof off before buckling down during the final stretch to the finish line next year.

The Glee kids trickled into the choir room in no particular rush. Having completed nationals, they really didn't have much to practice for. The only performance left was the end-of-year rally. No one cared too much about that.

Puck sat in the corner, casually strumming his acoustic guitar to what sounded like Alice Cooper's "School's Out." An enthralled Mike Chang sat on the steps nearby, flipping through Puck's copy of the McKinley High *Thunderclap*. Each page was bursting with suggestive notes and hastily drawn hearts. Mike's fingertips lingered on a phone number written in silver Sharpie, which took residence next to a smudged lipstick kiss.

"Dude, teach me your ways," said Mike as he marveled at a dirty letter from sophomore Cheerio Amanda Dunlap. It was so detailed that it took up the entire page — and made Mike's eyes bug out when he read it. Puck's brief stint in juvie hadn't really hurt his reputation at all. It might have even helped it. Chicks were into bad boys.

"Brosef, it only takes *one*. Get some chick to write 'I want you' somewhere noticeable, and the rest is cake. Girls love to compete. Especially when it comes to sluttiness," Puck explained, idly plucking the strings of his guitar. "I even got a few digits from dudes, too." His palms shot up in defense. "Not that I'm into that, but everyone *tries* with the Puckster." Puck punctuated the statement by winking at Quinn across the room. She folded her arms protectively across her body and turned to Sam, as if looking into his blue eyes could erase the memories of her and Puck's scandalous history.

"Can I, like...borrow your yearbook? To, um...sign it?" Brittany asked while fidgeting with what appeared to be a rabbit's foot key chain. She had traded with Lauren Zizes her chocolate cupcake for it. Lauren had told Brittany that if she planted it in her backyard, it would grow a real bunny. Brittany planned on naming it Zac Efron. She also hoped it would be at least half as cuddly.

"What did I tell you? Works like a charm." Puck yanked the *Thunderclap* out of Mike's hands and passed it to Brittany.

"Hey!" Mike protested as Tina gave him a light warning slap on the side of his head.

Brittany grabbed the book and skipped back to her seat. She plopped down, eagerly flipping it open to the club section to begin her annual ritual of defacing the New Directions group photo. It was strange because she herself was in it. Brittany carefully wrote the word *slut* over her own picture before moving on to draw a mustache on Rachel's perfect smile. Brittany giggled proudly, then started jotting down random phone numbers on her left forearm.

"Why aren't you entering those into your phone?" Tina asked. Brittany's motives for doing anything were always entertaining.

"Because my arm's always with me," Brittany replied in her hushed, monotonous voice.

Santana looked extremely bored. "Why are we here again? If something doesn't happen soon, I'm bouncing to get an iced cappuccino." She stifled a yawn.

"We are *here* because it is still the last week of school, which means Glee isn't over," Rachel butted in. "Some of us are committed to exercising our talents year-round, not just when it's *convenient*. Also, Mr. Schuester said he had an announcement."

Santana rolled her eyes and started inspecting her French manicure.

"Mr. Schu always has an announcement," Kurt pointed out. Several heads nodded in agreement. They were used to going along with Mr. Schuester's crazy schemes, but he always liked to make a big show of revealing whatever it was he had cooked up. He sought to keep them interested by using suspense, but it was mostly just annoying. Must have been the showman in him.

Rachel rose and marched to the front of the room. "While we are waiting, I also have something to share. I just wanted you all to know that this summer, I am —"

"Wow, now I'm *really* going," Santana interrupted as she

34

headed for the door, pulling a confused Brittany with her. "I'm so not into sad stories. And this sounds like one. As in, your life — it's sad."

That didn't really hurt Rachel's feelings, but it just proved her point further. *Santana will never have what it takes to be a star,* she thought. *Not like me.* She cleared her throat and began again. "As I was saying, before I was so rudely interrupted — I have designed an intensive summer schedule for myself that includes training in everything one needs to become a full-fledged star." The sea of blank faces did not deter her.

Rachel adjusted the strap of her sundress and continued. "Why am I telling you this? Not because I want you to do the same. I know you won't. I will continue to be the bar to which all of you are measured."

At this, Mercedes emitted a loud scoff. *How does someone become so conceited? Rachel should be studied,* she thought.

"Anyway, I just wanted to invite you all to the ballroom-dancing exhibition that Finn and I will be in at the end of the summer. He's taking classes with me." A chorus of laughs filled the room.

Finn's stomach lurched. *What has Rachel gone and done now?* He felt as if a bucket of ice water had been dumped over his head. It was a familiar sensation. Some of the guys had drenched him once after a football game, the first time Coach Beiste had finally led the Titans to a victory. But even that had felt sort of good, because they had won and stuff.

But now Finn was at a loss. This was the first he'd heard of any sort of dancing class. *Why do girls always plan crap without asking?* Finn wondered. Just a few minutes ago, he was happily spacing out, thinking about cheat codes on all the video games he had been neglecting of late. He had also mapped out all the sleeping and eating cereal in his sweatpants that he was going to do. Maybe even some basketball at the park with Puck. But, nope, no dancing class.

Finn's one summer obligation (which he already was trying to get out of) was a "family bonding" road trip to Graceland with his mother and the Hummels. His mother had always loved Elvis, and apparently so had Burt Hummel. Kurt was clearly in it for the rhinestone costumes. But Finn was not looking forward to spending hours upon hours crammed into the backseat of his mother's car while "Hound Dog" played on repeat. Now he had *two* miserable things to weasel his way out of without hurting anyone's feelings. Just great.

Rachel really was an evil mastermind. By announcing her surprise in front of a group, she must have thought he would agree to it on the spot so he wouldn't embarrass her. It was the same reason that men proposed to women in crowded restaurants or ice rinks. Finn was a little perturbed. Most people didn't put up with Rachel's presumptuous acts, but she often took advantage of his soft spot for her. But this time, it was so not cool. Come to think of it, he was pretty sure that she'd promised she was never going to pull something like this again, whether they were together or not. A public humiliation for personal gain thing, that is. *Oooh, maybe I can use that against her,* Finn thought as a smile formed on his lips. Rachel smiled innocently back at him.

Puck could hardly contain himself. "Dude, do you have to wear those nut-hugger pants? I heard they make your junk smaller."

Finn slumped in his chair.

Rachel tried to read Finn's weird body language as she took her seat next to him. Why didn't he look excited? Peculiar.

"All right, all right, everyone, let's calm down," Mr. Schuester said as he briskly entered the choir room. Brittany and Santana followed, looking like two children who'd been caught stealing from the cookie jar. Santana plopped back down in her seat and crossed her arms.

"Okay, so I know you are all excited to be finishing your classes, but I still need you guys to focus." Mr. Schuester looked a little too happy. It was the classic look of a teacher who was about to have a long vacation, Tina concluded. Maybe he was going to take that trip back to New York with his friend Bryan Ryan to see a bunch of Broadway shows. Then again, it could have just been all that vitamin D he was soaking in. Tina understood. Even though her personal style looked as if she would much prefer to spend her days in a dark coffin than a field of daisies, she was always happier when the sun came out.

"Now, I know that we had been practicing the 'Airplanes' mash-up. You guys sounded great, but I think we should go back to the drawing board for Friday's rally performance. Maybe something a little...fresher. Any ideas?" Mr. Schuester bit his lip. Delivering bad news made him really nervous.

"Ah, *hell* no!" Mercedes stood up. "That's not fair. I've been working on that song for weeks!"

It seemed Mr. Schuester could never please everyone. He had given up that battle long ago. "Mercedes, I'm truly sorry. But this will all make sense in a minute," Mr. Schuester said as he shook his head.

Typical, Mercedes thought. She felt like she was always fighting for her voice to be heard. *I wonder what it would be like to be the leader of something.* Whatever. She at least deserved to know what exactly had ousted her solo. "Spill it, Schuester," she said, jutting her hip out and putting her hand on it. She meant business.

In the far back, Sam Evans fidgeted. Sometimes, the way Mercedes interrogated people reminded him of his mother when she was angry. Everyone seemed to argue a lot in Glee Club—though he wasn't really sure why he had been surprised when he discovered that a club based on dramatic performance was full of drama, both onstage and off. At least the arguments in here didn't consist of grunting and insulting one another's moms, like with the football team. He pictured Rachel Berry in a "yo mama"–off with Tina Cohen-Chang. It was silly enough to make him forget the awkward scene playing out in front of him.

"A few weeks ago, Rachel approached me with some concerns," Mr. Schuester began.

"There's a shocker," Kurt muttered under his breath.

"She told me about the lack of opportunities in Lima for you to keep practicing during the summer," Mr. Schuester continued. Rachel's expression became increasingly smug. "It got me thinking — a lot of you probably feel the same way."

Now Mercedes was intrigued. For once, she might actually agree with Rachel. What was next — a downpour of locusts? Floods? Because this definitely seemed like the beginning of some sort of apocalypse.

"At first I thought that everyone could audition for the Lima Community Musical," Mr. Schuester said. "But unfortunately we all know that the auditions are practically rigged by the members of Vocal Adrenaline."

He was right about that. Kurt had tried out last summer, only to be stopped six bars into "Mr. Cellophane" (his old go-to number) with the one phrase a performer never wants to hear at an audition: "Thank you for coming."

Mr. Schuester rolled up the sleeves of his button-down shirt. "So... I worked really hard to find something for you guys. And, well, I didn't want to say anything until I had confirmed it with the elementary schools but" — he paused for effect — "there is going to be a McKinley High Summer Youth Music Camp this year!" Mr. Schuester stretched his arms out as if he were a magician who'd just pulled a rabbit out of a hat. The news hung stale in the air.

Santana finally broke the silence. "And this involves us *how?*" she snapped grumpily. Clearly, someone had been deprived of her caffeine fix.

Mr. Schuester's smile widened. "Well, that's the best part. *You* guys are going to be the counselors! You are going to coach the kids and help them put on performances. We could even have a mini mash-up day. It's going to be so great!" He looked around for some sort of reaction. There was a little less enthusiasm than he had hoped. "You guys are in, right?"

"Well, I am," Artie chimed in. "I like kids—we see eye to eye." He wasn't joking. Kids were usually around the same height as Artie when he was in his wheelchair. He sometimes got sick of staring up at everyone. Also, he found summer without Glee Club sort of boring. Of course, every year Artie always had lots of big ideas about new hobbies he could take up during the summer months. They never really came to fruition, though. It would definitely be nice to have something planned other than the usual pattern of sitting at home and watching *Battlestar Galactica* DVDs he would inevitably fall into by mid-July.

"That's the spirit." Mr. Schuester put his hand on Artie's shoulder. "This is the perfect opportunity for you guys to give back to the community and help some underprivileged kids have some fun. Plus, don't forget, young minds are very impressionable. Maybe we can even recruit some future New Directions members!" Mr. Schuester had seen this as one of his main selling points with the group. They had all worked so hard to lift the club up from the trenches in the past few years. Surely they wouldn't want to see it fall to pieces after they graduated. That had happened to *him* once before, and it didn't feel good. He looked around. "Come on, guys! Is Artie still the only one with me?"

Kurt considered what Mr. Schuester had said about giving back to the community. This would technically be seen as helping others, right? "Kids generally don't dress well. They smell funny and have tiny hands. But sign me up, and somebody tell my dad," Kurt said, thanking his lucky stars for such a prompt answer to this morning's dilemma. He then slid the unlock button on his touch-screen phone, logged on to his favorite shopping blog, and stopped listening.

The same point had resonated with Puck, who still owed several hours of community service for his court sentence. It was part of his post-juvie deal. "I'll do it. Does this, like, count as real service? Because the last time I tried to help a cripple, they said it didn't count and stuff." He popped a toothpick into his mouth and started chewing on it.

Mr. Schuester sighed. Maybe he should reconsider who was going to be allowed near the impressionable young minds. Still, he needed everyone in the club to sign up. Younger kids could be an even bigger handful than moody teenagers. "You really have got to stop using that word, Puck. Artie is a person. But yes, it should."

"Sweet deal."

Mercedes had already decided to join a few minutes ago, but she wanted to keep Mr. Schuester on the edge of his seat. She didn't agree with her solo's being taken away, so she was staging a silent protest. Mr. Schuester looked straight at her, all hopeful.

"What do you say, Mercedes?" His smile melted her icy shield.

"Fine. But it's only because I want to prevent those little girls from becoming Cheerios," she offered.

"Well, in that case," Quinn piped in, "I'm in, too. Unlike Mercedes, I want to teach them that they can do *all* the things they want to do in high school." Her golden curls bounced as she spoke, which usually happened when she was fired up. "Plus, they should at least know that they would be entering into a slushie-covered existence in Glee."

Sam quickly followed suit, not at all provoked into joining by the sharp kick Quinn delivered to his left shin or anything.

One by one, the rest of the club agreed to spend a major portion of their summer helping out at Mr. Schuester's camp. Everyone had different reasons. For Tina and Mike, it was nostalgia. They had spent the previous summer together as counselors at an Asian camp, and it was actually how they'd started dating in the first place. It might be cute to try it again. Like a little "campiversary." And this camp's lunch probably wouldn't consist of soup with chicken feet in it, which Tina had hated with a fiery passion.

Santana caved to avoid having to babysit her little cousin Lola all summer long while her aunt worked. The kid could be such a pain. Santana discovered this the hard way last summer when she and Brittany had spent an entire afternoon tied together with a Hello Kitty jump rope as the little girl's "prisoners." When Kurt pointed out that Santana was going to be looking after *many* children instead of just one, she replied, "Duh. You are forgetting about the obvious perk: hottie dads." Her unwavering goal to meet cute boys continued to astound those around her. Brittany usually fell in line with Santana, so no one was surprised by her decision to join up.

"I think it will be fun dressing up our new little onions. Maybe some in, like, gnome outfits. Because gnomes are little. And children are little." Somehow, Brittany's sentences always managed to come out like the haiku poems they had written in English class last semester—they usually didn't make much sense and left the audience to fill in the gaps.

"Do you mean 'minions,' Britt?" Kurt asked.

Brittany giggled. "No, silly, I'm pretty sure gnomes don't have cold hands. But they do wear hats." She thought Kurt knew stuff about fashion. Kurt dropped his face into his palms, emitting a loud smack. He didn't even know why he continued to try with that girl.

There were only two holdouts left. Mr. Schuester turned to Finn and Rachel, who had been uncharacteristically quiet during the whole conversation. Everyone knew that if there was one thing to fear, it was a silent Rachel. It usually meant a storm was coming. Sure enough, Rachel's mouth twitched a little at the corners. It was one of the early warning signs. "We can't do it without you guys," Mr. Schuester begged. He hoped to appeal to Rachel's need to be needed.

"Of course we will, Mr. Schu," Finn answered for the both of them. Clearly, he was eager to abandon Rachel's inspired dance-class plan. Maybe he could even get out of the dumb road trip to dumb Elvis's house, too. Besides, he and Rachel were practically the Glee team captains. How would it look to the rest of the group if they didn't join up, too?

"Speak for yourself, Finn." Rachel's tone was laced with the verbal equivalent of poison. "I, for one, will not be spending my summer teaching a bunch of misbehaved brats the words to a Miley Cyrus song. I have much better things to do with my time."

Mr. Schuester was puzzled. Hadn't Rachel been the one asking him for some outlet to perform this summer? She had practically begged, and for once, he had listened. Now she was the one student who didn't want to participate?

"Don't look so shocked, Mr. Schu. If you had bothered to look over the Star Power Summer calendar I so generously provided you with, you would know that I have a very tight schedule. You would also know that I've even secured a meeting with *the* Hayes-Carson Agency for Stage Actors! They don't take interviews with just anyone. I mean, it's on *Broadway.*" Rachel puffed up with pride.

"Do you mean this?" Mr. Schuester rummaged through his folders and held up a piece of paper that was covered in multicolored boxes and glittery stickers. "I found this in my mailbox in the main office. I thought it was a joke."

Santana snickered. She loved when Rachel got dissed by anyone, but it was especially funny when it was a teacher.

"Working hard to make your dreams come true is no joke.

But you know what is? All of you." Rachel calmly gathered her things, shooting daggers at Finn all the while.

Nobody tried to stop her. They had witnessed this scene several times throughout the school year, so no one really paid much notice to her tantrums anymore. She was like the girl who whined wolf. For Rachel Berry, it was all about the grand entrances and exits. She turned on her glittery red ballet flat and made for the door. Her long, dark hair whisked behind her.

"I hope you all have a fun summer with your glorified babysitting," she added before making a swift final exit.

"Looks like we just got some practice," said Mercedes as soon as Rachel was out of earshot.

Quinn shook her head in disgust. "That girl is unbelievable."

Mr. Schuester had bigger fish to fry than a hissy fit. He turned to the rest of the group. "So, what song should we sing for our future campers at the rally on Friday? They're coming to hear us perform."

She may not have been there to hear it, but apparently the show *did* go on, with or without Rachel Berry.

four

Breadstix restaurant, Monday evening

Would you like another root beer?" the bored-looking blond waitress asked Finn. She was pretty much the only waitress who ever worked at Breadstix. She raised her eyebrows at him quizzically. He was trying to fold a straw wrapper into the shape of a ninja star, like he'd seen Puck do once. He was failing at it.

"Oh, uh…not yet. Thanks." He'd sucked the first one down at record speed. Finn hated confrontation, and whenever he knew he was about to have a difficult conversation, his mouth got extremely dry. Waiting for Rachel to show up after her epic scene in Glee Club that afternoon had him particularly parched. It brought back memories of the time he got his wisdom teeth pulled and Dr. Howell had dressed his mouth with cotton balls. Finn gulped down the free glass of tap water the waitress had delivered along with the soda. He felt a little better. He should probably stop drinking so much soda, which his mother was always telling him to.

His mom usually gave pretty good advice. Taking Rachel to Breadstix for dinner that night was even her idea. She said that sometimes, when girls got upset about things, they just needed a little reminder to show them that you weren't a jerk—a nice gesture. He thought she had a point. Even though he totally didn't *have* to invite Rachel to dinner or anything, he hated being at odds with anyone. At least their crazy history had given him an advantage when dealing with her outbursts. All it took was a little coddling, really. Tonight, Finn was willing to "take one for the team" and calm her down. No one had asked him to. But Finn was that sort of guy—he just did nice stuff.

Also, maybe Finn did feel the tiniest bit guilty that he hadn't really stuck up for her earlier. Good thing he had a little money saved from his grandmother's annual birthday check. Maybe later, when she was filled up on her favorite Bottomless Salad Bowl, he could even try to persuade her to ditch her psycho summer plan and be a counselor at Mr. Schuester's youth camp.

Finn plucked a few breadsticks from the basket on the table. He bit into one, but it was so stale that it crumbled down the front of his shirt, leaving a trail of prickly crumbs everywhere. It didn't even really taste that good. Maybe it was time Lima found a new "it" restaurant. The scent of garlic hung heavily in the air, and the lighting was adjusted just low enough to mask whatever stains the carpet was sporting.

He looked around anxiously. The place was pretty empty, being a Monday night and all. The only patrons dining besides him were an elderly couple slowly eating minestrone soup in a corner booth and a young mother and her toddler at the adjacent table. The boy was smearing marinara sauce all over the table like he was finger painting, while the mother was trying to wipe his face. Every time she got close, he emitted a high-pitched shrieking sound.

Finn winced as he tried to ignore the awful noise. How did kids manage to hit the exact note that made the little hairs stand up on his arms every time? Even Rachel couldn't hit notes as consistently as this kid. Though maybe the goose bumps Finn was experiencing were a combination of the shrieking and the air-conditioning, which was on full blast. The restaurant was probably overcompensating for the hot summer weather outside. Lima could get pretty hot, even at night.

Finn's eyes darted to the door. Rachel wasn't mad enough at him to stand him up, right? That would blow. He'd given up cheeseburger night at home for this. Finn took the two half-eaten breadsticks and started practicing an awesome drum solo on the table. Recently, he'd found some of Burt Hummel's old Genesis records in the basement. Those guys weren't too bad. Especially the drummer, Phil Collins, who he'd thought was just a singer whom soccer moms and grandmas were into. Probably because his mom and grandma were into him. But the dude had mad drumming skills.

He was just finishing up a sweet breadstick/water glass rendition of "Invisible Touch" when Rachel appeared in front of the table. She was wearing a short blue dress covered in white polka dots, fiery red lipstick, and an expression of disdain. Finn scrambled to stand up. That's what you were supposed to do when a chick arrived, right? Or was that just with princesses? Finn wasn't sure, so he did it anyway.

She still seemed pretty ticked off. Finn wished he'd gotten that second root beer. "I'd, uh...pull out your chair for you but..." he stammered as he gestured to the booth.

"Sit down, Finn." Rachel had to work extra hard to stay mad at him. He was so cute when he was trying to be chivalrous. She gathered her shiny brown tresses to one shoulder and slid into the booth across from him. He sat wide-eyed and looking the very definition of innocent. Still, she reminded herself, he'd clearly asked her on this date because he felt he had something to apologize for. Well, he did. But Rachel figured she might as well enjoy dinner before addressing the elephant in the room. It wasn't too often that a high school boy paid for a meal.

The waitress came back around, and Finn ordered for the two of them. Rachel didn't normally like letting someone else take the reins, but she wanted to see if Finn would choose the right dish for her. She liked creating little tests for people in her mind. It was one of the best ways to judge a person. That afternoon's incident had been one test that Finn had failed. At least he knew that she liked to avoid carbs, she considered as Finn ordered her favorite salad.

"Feeling better?" Finn asked as he cleaned the last of his spaghetti and meatballs off his plate and stifled a burp. It had taken him about five minutes to polish it off.

Rachel picked at a suspicious-looking spinach leaf with her fork and looked up at him. She decided to go for it. "I know you were hoping that this date was going to make up for the fact that you totally hurt me today, but it doesn't." Her fork clanked loudly as she dropped it in her bowl. "And I can't believe you answered for me when Mr. Schuester asked if we would join his ridiculous camp!"

The little boy at the next table threw his sippy cup on the floor and screeched.

Finn hated to point out the hypocrisy in Rachel's last statement, but he couldn't help himself any longer. "It wasn't *anything* like you signing me up for some stupid ballroom-dance class without asking me, was it?"

Finn did have a point there. Not that she would admit it. "That was supposed to be a surprise. A fun thing to do and a way to improve your dancing skills," Rachel shot back. "I thought you would like it."

Finn wasn't buying that one. Rachel knew that choreography was one of his least favorite parts of Glee Club. Granted, he'd gotten better at it in the past few years, but it still wasn't his idea of a cool way to spend his downtime. He suspected that Rachel's "surprise" element of it all was pretty much so that he'd have a hard time saying no to her. "You know how I feel about dancing, Rachel. Come on. Admit that it was a gift for you, not me."

Rachel narrowed her eyes and crossed her dainty arms over her chest. He noted the absence of her gold-plated FINN necklace, which still made appearances from time to time depending on Rachel's mood, the day of the week, or where they stood with each other. "I will do no such thing. And don't try to persuade me to cancel all my classes and auditions to be a counselor with you guys, either."

Man, she's good, Finn thought. "How did you know I was about to do that?"

Rachel sighed heavily, clearly exasperated by having to explain something so simple to such an ignoramus. "I don't know why it's so hard for everybody to accept my talents and my intent to nurture them. Even naturals like me have to hone their skills, Finn. I simply cannot be expected to make any progress in my burgeoning career while looking after a crowd of whining children all summer."

The little boy at the next table burst into tears, and the mother frantically tried to quiet him with a toy helicopter. Rachel raised her eyebrows as though this random act had somehow illustrated her point about what little monsters children were.

The waitress appeared and began clearing their empty plates. "Any dessert for you kids? Some chocolate ice cream? Tiramisu?" Finn's mom always ordered the tiramisu, and he usually finished it off for her after she started complaining about how many calories were in it. It was pretty tasty. All those layers of cream and chocolaty stuff.

"Yeah, some of that," Finn responded, grabbing Rachel's uneaten Parmesan roll off her plate before it disappeared with the waitress for good. "And two spoons," he called after her, flashing two fingers on his hand.

Finn thought Rachel was being extremely selfish. "I know, but don't you ever want to give back? You could, like, nurture someone else's talents for once."

He sounded like Mr. Schuester, reciting some stupid speech and acting all noble and self-important. Finn chomped the rest of the roll and continued talking with a full mouth.

"I think it would be kind of sweet to see you teaching some tiny versions of yourself to sing."

He clearly wasn't getting it. Rachel wasn't going to budge on this one. Glee Club would just have to survive without her for the next three months. And if Finn continued to be such a jerk, he might have to as well.

Rachel slid out of the booth. "Well, maybe I'm not sweet. And you are completely missing the point. This summer is *my* time to shine." As she stood up, her skirt accidentally came up for a split second. Finn couldn't help looking and instantly forgot what they were arguing about. "Did you even listen to anything I just said?" Rachel asked a blank-faced Finn as she smoothed the fabric down. She hoped no one else had seen it ride up. The last thing she wanted to do was put on a peep show in a nice restaurant. The two of them had already been drawing enough attention with their

53

bickering. Earlier, she had sensed the pair in the corner watching them as if they were characters in a dinner theater production. The old couple probably didn't get out too much.

"Excuse me," the waitress said, shoving Rachel out of the way to make room for the massive square of tiramisu that was cleared for landing. She placed it in the center of the table, presumably for the two of them to share.

Finn outstretched a spoon toward Rachel. He seemed to finally notice that she was standing. "Are you leaving? We haven't even eaten dessert yet. Come on, sit down."

"If you had bothered to ask me, I would have told you that I don't like tiramisu." It was funny. Rachel thought she had come here tonight to receive an apology from Finn. Instead, all she'd gotten was more crap about the fact that she didn't want to work at Mr. Schuester's music camp. She needed to get out of there. "And, yes, I'm going home. Enjoy your dessert. Hope it's *sweet* enough for you."

She was out the door before Finn had even taken a single bite.

For the second time in the same day, Rachel Berry had made a grand exit. That had to be a record. As he ate his dessert in silence, Finn couldn't help but wonder if the show was over, or if there was a third act to this ridiculous production.

five

Lima Allen County Airport, Monday evening

Rachel scrambled up onto the hood of her little previously owned maroon Saturn. She'd parked in the fields near the Lima Allen County Airport, perfectly positioned to watch the takeoffs and landings (should there be any). It had been a long time since she'd come to this spot. When she was little, her dad Hiram went through a phase where he was really interested in all things aviation. He built model planes and painted names on the sides of them, just like the old war fighters used to. Except he would always dedicate his to his little princess, painting *The Beautiful Miss Berry* or *Rachel's Pride* on the wings. The letters usually looked pretty shaky, unlike the smooth script she had seen on the ones at the air show. But he tried.

From time to time, if they happened to pass the little

airport, they would stop and get out to watch the planes. Hiram would try to explain the mechanics of how things like wind speed affected the planes to Rachel and her other dad, Leroy, but they never understood it too well. Her favorite part was when they would play the game they'd dubbed "Where to? Where from?"

It was pretty much what it sounded like. A plane would take off—where to? A plane would land—where from? "Istanbul!" Hiram would yell. "Lima, Peru!" Leroy would joke. Rachel's answer was almost always "New York!" It was more than likely that the planes were just tiny commuter jets or private planes coming in from somewhere nearby, like Dayton, Ohio. But it was fun. She was lucky to have such great dads.

Rachel breathed in the warm evening air, which was filled with the sweet smell of freshly cut grass. The sun was finally starting to melt over the horizon, and the first stars began to peek through a buttery haze.

She was glad she had come here to get away from all the day's drama and just be alone. She'd been in such a great mood this morning, looking forward to her last week of junior year and a summer spent exactly the way she wanted. How had everything gone awry so quickly? She didn't appreciate being chastised for standing her ground in Glee Club. Dinner with Finn had been a disaster. Ugh. She didn't even want to *think* about any of it anymore. She hopped off the car and spread her gray cardigan on the ground like a picnic blanket so she didn't ruin her favorite blue dress.

Rachel mindlessly rolled a wayward blade of grass between her thumb and forefinger, leaving a green stain behind on her fingertips. It reminded her of the makeup the character Elphaba wore in the musical *Wicked*. She had read on her favorite website, Broadway Mania, that it took the actress who played the character more than an hour each night to put it all on. Rachel thought it must be hard to sit still for that long.

Lima, Ohio, was like the dressing room to the Broadway stage of her life — nothing more than a necessary precursor that she had to sit through to get to the first act. As soon as she had put in her time in hair and makeup, she would finally be able to step out and let the world see her. After this summer, it would be her turn to go onstage to perform for thousands at the Gershwin Theatre in New York. Or the Shubert. Or the Marquis. Really, any of them would do.

A small private jet touched down in the distance.

What sort of person owns a private jet? Rachel wondered if maybe it contained a big movie star being whisked into town to shoot some on-location scenes in scenic suburban Ohio. Yeah, right. Nothing exciting ever happened here. *When I'm a star, that's the only way I'm traveling,* Rachel decided. Even though her dads had gone to a movie and weren't home, she figured she should probably get going before it got dark. She was alone, after all.

A small, brown package awaited Rachel on the front doorstep when she got home. In all the craziness, she'd totally forgotten about the new pair of black character shoes she'd ordered. They were for the ballroom-dance class she was *supposed* to take with Finn. *What a waste.* She sighed and retrieved them from the ground. This brand was supposed to be the best—she had spent a massive chunk of time researching options online before choosing the right ones. It had been the recommendation of the ballroom-dancer-turned-television-star Julianne Hough that sealed the deal. But instead of being excited about opening them up and trying them on, Rachel felt they just seemed like a reminder of how things were not going according to her plan. And things should always go as planned.

Rachel needed some serious cheering up.

A few minutes later, a steamy pot of chamomile brewed while Rachel cozied up on the sofa with her copy of *Elements of Elocution.* Hot tea was always a good way to soothe one's vocal cords, even when the temperature outside matched that of the boiling liquid. Of course, Rachel probably needed it more today from all the yelling she'd done instead of actual vocal training. Well, that would change soon enough. She was about to purge her life of the exhausting characters she was forced to put up with on a daily basis.

They were all nuts, but Mr. Schuester was seriously delusional—maybe even the most insane of them all. It shouldn't have come as too much of a shock that he would piece together some last-minute, half-baked music camp for kids. Mr. Schuester was not only a softie, but he was also very impractical. Running a camp was going to be a ton of work. Rachel doubted that there would be much time for any serious vocal practice. Kids were so fussy. Didn't Mr. Schu know that one of the first rules of show business was to never work with children or animals?

That was the main reason Rachel didn't own a pet, even though it seemed to be yet another topic in which she held a controversial opinion. One time, Mercedes had told a story about how she had taught her dog, Sparkles, to lift its paw and shake Mercedes's hand. Mercedes had spent a whole weekend perfecting the trick, giving it treats and encouragement. Then, when she finally tried to show her family, the dog had totally forgotten the whole thing. How imprudent. Rachel didn't need that kind of drama in her life—though when she was seven, she did go through a brief Toto-coveting phase after far too many viewings of *The Wizard of Oz*. But she had come to her senses. Animals were so messy and required tons of care. Rachel had no time to be giving a smelly dog a bath. Or to be picking up after it. *Ew.*

"Pets are completely unnecessary," Rachel had piped in after Mercedes had finished her story. "I'd never want a dog."

Kurt had responded, "That's probably a good thing. You would totally be one of those owners who subject their pets to wearing hideous sweaters. Much like the one you're sporting right now." Rachel did have a weird obsession with knitwear emblazoned with animal silhouettes, and on that particular day, she'd worn a brown one bearing the outline of a white horse.

"Except it would have a human knitted on it," Mercedes had added amid a chorus of laughter.

Rachel poured some tea into her favorite *Phantom of the Opera* mug and blew on the surface to cool it down. Being alone was so nice. She cracked open her book and began the next chapter, titled "Modulation and Management of the Voice." She only had to read the first two sentences before it became very clear that this was not the antidote to her current distressed state. Something lighter was in order.

Funny Girl always lifted her spirits. She flicked on the television, excited about her new plan. Rachel loved the story of Fanny Brice, a misunderstood Jewish girl with big dreams of stardom. Fanny grew up surrounded by people who didn't believe in her talents, but she ultimately showed everyone up by becoming a huge star. It was eerily parallel to Rachel's life. And who didn't love Barbra Streisand? Barbra was one of twelve people in history who had achieved the "EGOT," winning all four of the most coveted accolades in entertainment: an Emmy, a Grammy, an Oscar, and a Tony. That was an accomplishment Rachel hoped would at one point be hers. She would be number thirteen.

Rachel was popping the DVD from its case when the TV caught her attention. "Coming up next: *Song and Dance: The Bernadette Peters Story*," the announcer bellowed. Rachel was rapt with attention as the program began. "Bernadette Peters has had a stunning career on both stage and screen that has spanned five decades, touching millions of hearts with her moving performances and spectacular vocals. The star began her career at the tender age of three and a half." Ha.

Rachel had won her first dance competition at a mere three *months* old.

The screen flashed a slideshow of old photographs as the announcer continued. "By age five, she had appeared on several national television shows and was well on her way to her first performance on the New York stage as Tessie in *The Most Happy Fella*, when she was only eleven years old." *Eleven years old?* These facts were not encouraging. Here she was, almost seventeen. And she hadn't even come close to her Broadway debut yet. How awful.

Her fingers scrambled for the remote and pushed hard on the power button. So what if Rachel had been at a disadvantage her whole life? She still had the talent and determination that others severely lacked. It simply wouldn't cut it to just sit here like a couch potato, like every other teenager in Lima. She had to do something now. As in, right this second.

Her feet couldn't climb the stairs to her bedroom fast enough. The brown box sat innocently on her bed, beckoning Rachel to open it. Completely disregarding her plans to send it back, she ripped off the packing tape and waded through the glittery tissue paper inside. The smell of new shoes permeated her nose. There was something about the smell of new stuff that was really exhilarating. Rachel breathed it in as she brought the right shoe up to her face for closer inspection. The heel sure looked a lot higher than it had in the pictures online. Rachel was more a ballet flats type of girl. She had an extensive collection of them in all colors and bearing embellishments from bows to flowers (and even some with ponies printed on them) to prove it. *Might as well try them on*, she thought, kicking off her left teddy-bear slipper.

It took a minute to buckle her feet in. They felt a bit snug, but Rachel ignored it. It was probably just the style. She stood slowly, wobbling like a newborn colt taking its first steps. Rachel could see her toes starting to turn white under the black strap. How did Julianne wear these every single night? *Ouch.*

She'd come this far, though. No point in wussing out now. Rachel took the plunge and spun around on the ball of her right foot. The turn quickly devolved into a stumble, and Rachel caught the frame of her four-poster bed just in the nick of time. There was a reason that ballroom dancing required two people. Maybe it was the shoes.

But Rachel was not one to give up that easily. She spent the next ten minutes waltzing around her room, trying to perfect the few moves she already knew from some easy partnering routines in Glee Club. She could totally do this without Finn. Maybe she would even get partnered with some random cute guy whose grandmother had forced him into taking classes. They would be the star couple of the class, picking up on everything twice as fast as the others. The instructor would turn to them every time he wanted a combination demonstrated. Naturally, others would get jealous and try to bring her down by pushing her to the back of the room. "Nobody puts Rachel in a corner!" her partner would say as he scooped her up into his arms, spun her around, and dipped her back.

Or maybe she'd seen *Dirty Dancing* one too many times.

Da-dum! An instant-message window popped up on her computer desktop, obscuring the Photoshopped screen-saver of herself holding two Grammys. From across the room, Rachel could make out the flashing screen name: Sharkfinn5.

It was Finn.

That handsome, strapping...complete jerk of a leading man. She really ought to ignore him. She deserved an apology in the form of Finn holding a bouquet of red roses on her doorstep. Not a crappy instant message. *I won't respond. I'll just click out of it and sign off,* Rachel reasoned, trying to pretend that she wasn't interested in what he had to say for himself. Another message came through. *Da-dum.* In truth, she was dying to read it. *Da-dum, da-dum.* The chat window blinked furiously.

Completely forgetting about her precarious footwear, Rachel leaped toward her desk. It was a bad choice, considering the uncharacteristically messy state of her room. The floor was now littered with the remains of the packaging. Glittery tissue paper was everywhere. Her teddy-bear slippers sat abandoned by the foot of the bed.

Somehow, Rachel's foot found the worst spot ever to land. The heel of her right shoe caught the ear of her left slipper. It was over. She teetered for a millisecond before clumsily fall-ing headfirst into her bust of Patti LuPone. *Crash!*

As Rachel fell to the ground, she swore she could see tons of glittery, shining stars....

Then everything went black.

six

Interior of jetBerry plane, at some point in the future, Monday afternoon

Da-dum. Rachel's head throbbed something awful. What...happened? As she tried to blink herself awake and recall the events that caused her to lose consciousness, visions of golden sparkles filled her eyes. She must have hit her head really hard. Her feet still felt cramped, too. Steadying herself slowly, Rachel sat up, and the room around her came into sharp focus. Or rather, the interior of a plane did.

She was not in her colorful red-and-yellow bedroom in Lima at all. Instead, she appeared to be inside a luxurious private jet that was decked out in the finest furnishings. She felt the smooth leather chair that cradled her, realizing that she occupied one of four cushy black leather recliners. They had gold piping and were embroidered with the airline logo, a gold star. What a coincidence! That was Rachel's symbol, too.

Rachel began to drink in the spectacle with a newfound curiosity.

A little table opposite her bore a spread of delicious food. Fresh berries littered trays of fluffy croissants, and little star-shaped pats of butter accompanied them. Rachel wasn't even hungry, but her mouth watered at the sight. Flat-screen televisions playing *Funny Girl* hung on each wall. An elaborate arrangement of orchids—her favorite flowers—filled the air with a sweet fragrance. And there was Kurt, standing over her, wearing a gold blazer with a classic black skinny tie. He would look like a fifties game show host if it weren't for the fact that he had accessorized the getup with a ridiculous-looking brown hat and an expression of apathy. Wait—what was Kurt Hummel doing here?

Before Rachel could ask for any sort of explanation, Kurt interrupted, as if he could read her thoughts. "Are you finished with your deer-in-headlights, Dorothy-from-*The-Wizard-of-Oz* bit? Because I really need you to focus and tell me whether this Christian Siriano will do for the McKinley High performance." He dangled an avant-garde gold sequined minidress in front of her. "Or do you want something flashier...or sluttier?" It looked more like something Rihanna would wear than Rachel, who had a penchant for sporting clothes that made her look like a five-year-old librarian. This must have been the glittery thing clouding her vision earlier.

Kurt ignored the frightened look on Rachel's face and continued to babble on about outfit options. "There's also a Badgley Mischka that could work. You are really flat-chested, of course, so I —"

Da-dum! Thankfully, a loud noise interrupted what was about to be a thorough rundown of Rachel's biggest insecurities. An image of a seat belt lit up on the ceiling. "Welcome back to Ohio, Ms. Berry," the pilot announced over the intercom. "We'll begin initial descent into Lima shortly. Buckle up and enjoy the rest of the ride. Must be good to be home." Kurt plopped down in one of the leather recliners and clicked the lap belt securely into place. He seemed extremely put out at not being able to flit around the cabin, grabbing gowns of various colors and holding them up next to Rachel's skin to see the effects of each.

Welcome back? Rachel pondered. *When did I ever leave?* She didn't want to ruin the moment by asking, but she couldn't bear it any longer. This was all so surreal. The plane. The gold stars everywhere. The things Kurt was saying about performances. It almost seemed like . . .

"Kurt — is this *my* plane? Am I finally . . . a star?" Her brunette hair fell in cascades around her tiny frame, making her look like a doll. Her wide-eyed expression added to the effect.

Kurt ignored her. She creeped him out when she seemed like a tiny child. Which was surprisingly often.

Before she could ask another question, a tall steward who resembled some sort of Nordic prince approached them with a platter of just-warmed towels. He was so hot that it was hard to tell whether the steam was rising from the white cloths or him. His gold uniform matched the flaxen shade of his perfectly parted hair, and he wore one of those enameled pins with the wings on each side. Instead of an airline that she'd heard of before, this one bore the name *jetBerry.* Below it was *Defying Gravity* — clearly a nod to the show tune of the same name.

"Thank you, Anders," Kurt said, not so slyly giving him the once-over as he accepted a towel from a pair of gilded tongs. He reluctantly tore his eyes away from the object of his affection and turned them back to Rachel.

"I'm never letting you take those motion-sickness meds again. You'd think someone with her own jet would have gotten used to flying by now." He patted his face gently with the hot towel. "Honestly, you are worse than Drew Barrymore in *50 First Dates* with your ridiculous questions." The words were muffled as Kurt reclined, taking full advantage of the benefits of the washcloth. Recycled air wreaked havoc on your pores, and they had been in the air for a few hours.

"Was it that one where it's last summer and you are, like, dancing in your bedroom in some ugly, super-high shoes again? That must have been a really epic moment for you if you keep reliving it."

Up until now, Rachel had thought that this must have all been some ridiculously fantastic dream. But it wasn't. It was the other way around. Rachel felt like she was going to explode with excitement. She unbuckled her seat belt, even though the sign was still lit up. It was her plane, after all. She could do whatever she wanted.

"So it's true? I'm a Broadway star?" Rachel popped a raspberry into her mouth. It tasted even better than she'd anticipated.

Kurt rolled his eyes. Clearly, this was his least favorite part of Rachel's amnesia episodes. "Yeah, yeah. You're famous. People love you. Et cetera, et cetera, et cetera." Kurt often quoted *The King and I* to make fun of Rachel. She was oblivious to it, even though she was acting as if she were royalty now. "What else do you want to know, Your Majesty?"

Rachel had a million questions she wanted answered. Where to start? "Tell me...what show am I in?" Her eyes sparkled like those of a giddy child who had just been told she was on her way to Disneyland for the first time. She crossed over to the back of the plane, eager to explore all the delights of her new life. She picked up a short, one-shouldered chiffon dress in a bold shade of cerulean. It had been spread out on top of a stack of several other designer dresses of varying colors and silhouettes. All of these were for *her*. She giggled.

Kurt scribbled something in a leather-bound notebook that seemed to be bursting with fabric samples and neon sticky notes. He was only partially paying attention to her now. He seemed to have a lot on his plate.

Obviously, Rachel was boring him with this trite routine. He glanced up at her in a way that confirmed he thought she was completely nuts. *She should really get a CAT scan or something*, he thought. How was it possible that someone who was able to memorize tons of lines and perform them each night for a packed theater couldn't even remember what show she was in? Maybe karma was finally catching up with her. She'd had an incredible amount of good luck for someone who was so insufferable all the time. "A revival of *Oklahoma!* at the Imperial. You're costarring with Meredith Stewart from that show on the CW about teenage murderesses or whatever. And that guy Carmine Bennett. He's from some boy band—" He interrupted himself. "That color makes your skin look yellow."

Rachel quickly dropped the blue gown, allowing it to slide through her fingers and into a delicate heap on the carpeted floor. She began to hyperventilate.

"I'm Laurey?" she squealed between gulping large breaths of air. It was one of the three roles that she had always known she was destined to play. The other two were Eva Perón in *Evita* and, obviously, Fanny Brice in *Funny Girl*. It was almost too much to take in. She felt faint.

As if by magic, Anders appeared at her side, producing a goblet of cold water. "Ms. Berry," he offered with a flirty wink. My goodness, she could get used to service like this. This was all better than it had ever been in her dreams when she lived back in Podunk Lima. The sexy flight attendant was an excellent addition.

Lima! The pilot said something about it before. "Are we stopping in Ohio to refuel before continuing on to Los Angeles for an awards ceremony? Am I nominated or just performing?" Rachel blinked innocently at Kurt. His face sure was scrunching up strangely. Sort of like Mr. Schuester's used to when she would make suggestions for songs they could sing at regionals. Thank goodness that was all behind her now. "Kurt! I need to know if I should have a speech prepared. I do have one that I've been saving for my first Tony... but maybe I can change it before we fly back to New York?" Rachel had watched every Tony Awards on television since she was born. And even a few from before she was born.

"Look, I don't understand what's going on with you right now, Rachel. You are scheduled to perform at McKinley High's end-of-year rally this week." Kurt took out some dental floss and started to work on his perfectly straight teeth. He was apparently still just as obsessed with personal hygiene as she was. He also didn't care that he had obviously just rocked her entire world.

"Oh. Well, maybe my show premiered too late in the season." That was odd. She had definitely planned to be nominated for her role as Laurey. "You seem to have all the answers. Why are you here, again?" Kurt's lack of enthusiasm for all she had accomplished was starting to grate on her.

"I'm your costume designer *slash* life coach *slash* only person who will put up with you." Kurt yawned and peeked out the oval-shaped cabin window. "After you skipped town to go have your little Mary Tyler Moore moment, I decided that big-city life was my destiny, too. That youth music camp was *so boring.* Plus, there was that whole thing with Santana. Anyway, I just sort of... underestimated how many young

71

gay guys there were trying to break into the musical-theater scene." There was more than a hint of bitterness behind his voice. "This is just my interim gig until I get my big break. Which I totally will.

"But boy, do you *need* me." Kurt gestured to the mounds of expensive clothes that littered every available surface. "Thanks to my genius, you finally don't look like you've made the finals in the Scripps National Spelling Bee for a record-breaking eighth year." It was true. Rachel did have an unhealthy obsession with kneesocks. "A couple of months ago, I spent a whole twenty minutes outside the theater, trying to convince a chaperone from a middle school tour that you were not one of his students. He couldn't believe you weren't a thirteen-year-old visiting the city with your class from Tenafly, New Jersey."

Rachel suddenly became aware of her own reflection in a nearby mirror. Her current outfit consisted of a gauzy white blouse, a soft aqua lightweight scarf, and dark denim skinny jeans. Delicate gold bangles matched her metallic gladiator sandals and completed the look. She hadn't even noticed the chic yet comfortable ensemble until now. "Hello, gorgeous," she said to the mature brunette staring back at her. Damn, Kurt was good. Maybe she should wear pants more often.

Rachel crossed over to the other window and peeked out, brushing the silky, star-embroidered curtains aside to get a better look. A puzzle of interlocking green and brown pieces made up the landscape below. She wasn't afraid of heights.

Flying only made her nervous because of the whole takeoff and landing parts of it. She really would prefer not to become the next Buddy Holly, who should have had a very long career in the spotlight.

"Between dressing you and diffusing all the bad press, it's a full-time job."

"Bad press?" Rachel asked, her ears perking up. Surely he was joking.

"You have developed a reputation for being quite the diva. It's great—the tabloids even call you Scary Berry. I came up with that one myself. Isn't it brill? It's sort of an homage to the Spice Girls." Kurt sipped his goblet of water.

Well, haters were nothing new. They were probably just jealous. People were always mean when you had something they wanted. Rachel had experienced this phenomenon her entire life. Fame was a double-edged sword.

She struggled to process all the new information as the bustling metropolis of Lima, Ohio, came into view in the distance. She was famous. *Yay!* Kurt was her assistant. *Okay, fine.* She was going back...to Lima? *Weird.*

This McKinley High performance slightly puzzled Rachel. She had spent years trying to get *out* of Lima. Only last year, she had abandoned Glee Club for her Star Power Summer. It had clearly paid off. At the time, though, the whole club had done absolutely nothing to support her. Why would she ever want to go back to the place that hadn't understood her talents? There was only one logical reason—they all must have finally come to their senses! The kids at McKinley probably wanted to make it up to her by making the show a tribute to her success. Had to be it.

Rachel opened her mouth to confirm her new theory, but Kurt interrupted her, answering the question before she even had the chance to ask it. "You sort of invited yourself, actually. Who knows *why*..." She racked her brain for more details about the circumstances that had led her to this point. Maybe she was a humanitarian now, and this was all part of her constant need to give back to others. It *was* extremely nice of her to go back to McKinley and sing for the students after all they had put her through. Jeers. Laughs. *Slushies.*

Something told her that she would be greeted with different reactions this time around. As soon as she walked through the familiar doors of McKinley High School, there would be a tidal wave of applause and excitement at the return of their very own celebrity. Rachel would float down the hallway, ignoring autograph requests and scanning the crowd for her old friends from Glee Club.

The members of New Directions were going to be ecstatic at her arrival. They probably missed her so much. It must have been a huge struggle for them to compensate for the loss of her enormous talent. It was almost like when Beyoncé deserted Destiny's Child to pursue a solo career. She was clearly the one pulling all the weight. It was sad, but no one even remembered those other girls now. At least the people Rachel had left behind could find solace in the bragging rights they had earned having known her "way back when."

She pictured Mercedes begging her to sing a duet with her "for old times' sake." The Cheerios would ask her to make a cameo in their latest routine. And everyone else in the school would wish they could get a glimpse into "A Day in the Life" of Rachel Berry this year. It would certainly be a stark contrast to last year's embarrassing *Thunderclap* feature.

The plane hit a pocket of turbulence, knocking Rachel off her feet and into a pile of nearby dresses. As she clawed her way through the luxurious layers of silk and cashmere, she finally answered Kurt's question. "I think the gold dress will be perfect for the show. It doesn't need to be any sluttier — I'd like to let my talent speak for itself."

"Whatever you say, Princess," Kurt responded, signaling for Anders to help Rachel up from her couture nest. "But may I suggest you sit down? Things are about to get a lot bumpier than you think."

Rachel acquiesced, slouching back into the cushy baseball glove of a seat and buckling up. She smiled blissfully.

Little did she know, Kurt was talking about more than just turbulence. Rachel Berry was about to be in for a very rough ride.

seven

Chateau Lima Hotel, Monday evening

The Chateau Lima was well known among the Ohio elite for being the only acceptable hotel in the area. It had a nice, cavernous lobby that played soft piano music and made excellent use of lighting, and it employed a pretty good concierge. The hotel itself boasted ten stories, though most of the rooms were often vacant, unless there was an event going on. Sometimes a business convention or local beauty pageant was held in one of the ballrooms. Even the odd bat mitzvah might bring in guests. But for the most part, the venue was largely empty and out of place.

It was perfect, though, for when someone important came to town. He or she could usually be found occupying one of the hotel's two luxury penthouse suites. However, it was a rare occasion that a visitor to Lima fit this bill. As a result, the suites were still practically brand-new. On top of that, they boasted a view of the downtown — which was way better than the view of the power plant on the opposite side. Obviously, it was the only acceptable place for a star of Rachel's caliber to stay during her visit.

But when they pulled up in their limousine, Rachel's face dropped. "Oh, the Chateau."

Kurt looked at her blankly. "It's the best there is. You know that."

"Oh, it's not that. It's just...I was kind of excited to go home and see my dads," she said, staring out through the tinted glass of the hired vehicle. The inside smelled like fake pine and years of cigarette smoke.

The doorman standing at the entrance looked more like he belonged on Park Avenue than in northwestern Ohio. He wore white gloves and a top hat, but a drip of sweat on his face ruined the illusion. The poor man was boiling in his uniform in the early summer heat.

"Why aren't we staying at our houses?" Rachel thought it would be sort of quaint to stay in her old bedroom, to see all her little knickknacks and motivational posters that adorned the walls and had once acted as her own little cheerleaders. It would have been such a great moment. Too bad a documentary crew wasn't here to capture her emotional response at realizing how far she'd come. Maybe it wasn't too late to hire one.

"Oh God. Why do I always have to be the bearer of bad news? Just please don't go all Naomi Campbell and throw something at me like the last time...." Kurt said, loosening his collar. "Remember? I told you a few months ago that they sold the house."

"They *what*?" That hadn't been part of the plan. "Where ... where are they now?" All of a sudden, Rachel felt really young. "Did they move to New York to be with me?"

Kurt opened the door and climbed out, forcing her to follow him if she wanted more information. The doorman looked excited at the prospect of finally opening the door and letting a cool whoosh of air-conditioning escape. He smiled at them as he pulled the heavy gilded handle. "Good afternoon! Welcome to Chateau Li—" he tried to say, but the bickering duo paid him no mind as they entered the lobby.

"They wanted to, but *you* wouldn't let them. Or rather, you made it very clear that they were cramping your style."

Rachel whimpered like a puppy with a thorn stuck in its paw. "I would never do that. My dads are my biggest fans."

Rachel listened in disbelief as Kurt explained how Leroy and Hiram Berry would go to the theater each night. They would sit right up front, singing along to all the songs and wearing T-shirts that said RACHEL'S DADDY. They had been incredibly proud of her, just like always. Until Rachel told them to get lost.

Or rather, she'd insisted they "tone it down." Kurt said that Rachel became so caught up in being a Broadway professional, their presence completely humiliated her. She asked them whether they would stop coming to all the shows. They were so hurt by her request that they decided to come back to Lima. But it was too empty without her.

It wasn't long before they sold the house and used the money to take a trip around the world together. Hiram had always wanted to do it, and because Rachel no longer needed them, why not? They still loved her, of course. It was evident that she was always on their minds, as they made sure to send postcards and gifts from every destination they visited. They sent trinkets from all the exotic places they'd named while watching the planes take off when she was a little girl.

Rachel sat down on one of the lobby's plush camel-colored sofas, despair written all over her perfectly made-up face. "Where are their letters or postcards?" she asked, trying to comprehend the fact that she was alone. This was the first part of her new life that didn't seem so great.

Kurt grabbed her hand and pulled her up. He was growing more and more impatient with each passing minute. He was looking forward to checking into their suites and getting some quality rest before the next day. It was bound to be a doozy.

"I always just throw them out now. After they mailed you that coconut from Hawaii, you told me to never waste your time with their ridiculous gifts again." Rachel had actually catapulted the coconut at his head while in a rage. It was a special mood of hers that he fondly referred to as "Rage-el." She had the worst mood swings. "Of course, if they send something European, I usually just keep it for myself." It was one of the better perks of his job. "Come *on*. You clearly need some rest. And so do I. You are especially taxing today. This must be how Lindsay Lohan's rehab sponsor feels."

Rachel decided to just let Kurt take the reins. He got them

both checked into the two penthouse suites and was carting her luggage up to her room when it occurred to her to think about someone other than herself. "Don't you want to go stay with your family, Kurt? Just because I'm alone...doesn't mean you should have to be."

"Did you hit your head or something? Please go back to being your normal, bossy self. You're weirding me out." Kurt began the arduous task of unloading Rachel's twelve massive Louis Vuitton trunks. He grunted. "I'd yell at you for packing too much, but I packed it." He amused himself a little too much.

"Don't you want to see your dad...and Carole and... *Finn*?" Rachel sucked in her breath as if the name were sacred. It sort of was. What had become of Finn? Her heart ached a little at the very thought of him.

"Well, to put it lightly—they weren't thrilled when I dropped out of school to move to New York and follow in your footsteps. Especially after all that tuition money they spent on me at Dalton Academy." Kurt's dad and Finn's mom had given up their honeymoon to pay for Kurt's schooling. It was understandable for them to be upset. "Plus, everything is so churchy with Quinn around all the time." He dragged a trunk across the carpet.

Rachel's heart sank. "What do you mean?" Had Finn fallen back under Quinn's spell in her absence? *Please don't let it be true*, Rachel wished.

"Oh, whoops. I forgot you still carry a birthday candle-sized torch for Finn."

Rachel couldn't really deny that. Finn had been her real first love. Her only love, really. Theirs had been a rocky road, but the thought of him with another girl now made her sick with jealousy. "But as you know, my dear stepbrother really can't resist the 'Quinnfluence.' I still can't believe how religious he's gotten since getting back together with her. It's way more intense than that time he thought he saw Jesus's face in a grilled cheese sandwich."

This was not good. First her dads had abandoned her for some magical mystery tour around the world. Now Finn had gone back to Rachel's former rival — the one girl who was the absolute opposite of Rachel in every way. With her sugary-sweet demeanor, blond curls, heart-shaped lips, and little diamond cross necklace, how could anyone compare? Rachel couldn't believe that after all she had accomplished, she was starting to get jealous of Quinn again.

"Ew, you look awful," Kurt said, inspecting her. He had finally finished unloading the bags into her massive suite and was now standing in the doorway. He looked quite beat himself. His gold jacket was thoroughly wrinkled, and his hair had fallen flat outside in the hot weather. "Maybe it's just the face you're making. Remember what that face feels like ... and never make it again. Okay? You'll thank me later." Kurt could be terribly harsh, but at least he was honest. "Remember what I taught you about smizing. . . . It's just smiling with the eyes. Use it. Own it."

"Thanks, Tyra Banks." Rachel shoved Kurt out into the hallway. She really needed to get some rest.

"Get tons of sleep. We have an early meeting tomorrow at McKinley!" Kurt yelled as Rachel slammed the door in his face. Rachel thought she heard him say "We don't want you puffy!" but the door muffled his voice.

She turned around and took in the massive, empty suite before her. It was stunning. Well, stunning for a hotel in Lima. Rachel figured that she probably stayed in five-star hotels all the time now. But this one was decorated in rich jewel-toned fabrics and exotic-looking plants. A golden damask chaise lounge accompanied a teal velvet sofa and armchair that were covered in golden throw pillows. Lush purple curtains framed the large windows. Outside, the sun was starting to set, creating a vivid sky of colors. It looked like one of those desktop backgrounds you could download for your computer.

A giant, glittery abstract painting of what appeared to be a pair of ruby slippers hung above the mantelpiece. Everything about the room was beautiful, but the painting made her sad. It reminded her of all the times she'd watched *The Wizard of Oz* with her dads. *There's no place like home*, Rachel thought. She still wasn't quite over the fact that her house was no longer hers. It made her feel like an orphan. And not in the good way she felt when she sang Cosette's part in *Les Misérables*.

Everything would be much better in the morning. It was still early, but Rachel began to sift through one of the trunks, looking for anything that resembled sleepwear. She finally settled on a yellow lacy camisole dress — though it could have easily been a really slutty regular dress—and slipped into it. She shivered. They really pumped the air-conditioning at full blast in these places.

Rachel padded into the next room and drank in the sight of the king-size bed. She got a running start and dove onto the bed like a five-year-old. The soft, 800-thread-count white sheets enveloped her, and she snuggled in them.

As she tried to clear her mind and fall asleep, her thoughts kept turning back to Finn. Had he really gotten over her that easily? Was she really still in love with him? Maybe she just wanted what she didn't have. *Snap out of it, Rachel Berry,* she thought. Rachel was a big star now. She really didn't need the affections of some high school senior in Lima, Ohio. They lived in completely different worlds now, anyway. Still, a tiny part of Rachel hoped that Finn might just change his mind tomorrow when he caught a glimpse of her in all her glory—the new and improved (and Kurt-engineered) Rachel. Some old emotions would definitely get rustled up.

For the next few hours, Rachel drifted in and out of a restless sleep. No matter how she seemed to arrange herself in the gargantuan bed, she couldn't get comfortable. But Rachel knew it wasn't the bed. Her mind was in overdrive trying to process all that had happened to her in what had seemed to be just the past twenty-four hours. She had gone from dreaming of stardom in her childhood bedroom and having a silly fight with her boyfriend to being a jet-setter in her own private plane.

Rachel pinched her arm. *Hard.*

"Ouch!" she screamed out to no one at all. She looked around at the darkened room, expecting something to have magically changed. Nope. Everything looked exactly the same. Giant bed. Flat-screen television. Fancy lamp. Not home.

This was exhausting. Rachel flopped around like a fish out of water. Her stomach grumbled loudly. Ah, so she was just hungry. That was totally fixable! She fumbled for the light switch, excited to have something to do that was within her control. She located the room-service menu and gave it a quick once-over. There weren't too many options, though, and a goat cheese salad seemed like a weird choice in the middle of the night.

Maybe it was just a sense-memory, but Rachel suddenly developed an insane craving for a slushie. After all the years of torment she had suffered involving the frozen beverage, it even surprised her that she would want one. But she did. Really badly.

It didn't take her long to find a twenty-four-hour mini-mart near the hotel. The glowing fluorescent sign was even visible from a few blocks away, like a beacon. It felt really good to get outside and stretch her legs. She had been on the plane for so long and then spent the rest of the evening languishing on a bed the size of four Coach Beistes (and the McKinley football coach was a hefty woman). The summer air had finally cooled, and Rachel was pleased to be on a little adventure. She felt like she hadn't breathed in fresh air in ages. Her lungs had probably gotten used to the dirty environment of New York City.

Ding-dong. An electronic bell went off as she entered the small, run-down store. The old man sitting at the cashier's counter peeked out from behind his newspaper long enough to bow his head ever so slightly at Rachel, like some cowboy from a spaghetti-western movie.

"Good evening, sir." She smiled at him. He raised his eyebrow suspiciously, grunted, and went back to reading an article about a recent increase in cow-tipping crimes in the area. Apparently, Lima teenagers were really bored.

The loud yet familiar hum of the slushie machine in the corner overpowered the sound of the crackling portable radio on the counter. Rachel thought the song was "Here Comes the Sun" by the Beatles, but she couldn't be sure. The liquid churning around inside the machine was purple—which meant that it was grape! Grape had always been Rachel's favorite flavor to get slushied with back at McKinley. She would always lick her lips while washing her face in the girls' bathroom.

In the process, she had become quite the expert on slushie flavors. She could break down the pros and cons of each one like a sommelier in a fancy restaurant rambling on about the characteristics of different wines. She also knew which colors stained clothes the worst. For example, red was absolutely killer. Rachel had cried once after Dave Karofsky cherry-slushied her while she was wearing her white sweater with a yellow cat on the front. Unfortunately, the sweater did not have nine lives.

But that was all behind her now. Slushies were purely for her enjoyment, not an unexpected icy bath. Rachel chose a jumbo-size cup and filled it to the top with the bright purple liquid.

At the register, Rachel noticed the latest edition of *Superstar Weekly*—a trashy celebrity tabloid magazine that she used to often see Kurt or Mercedes devouring before the bell rang. Rachel didn't like to admit it, but she was also a fan. Looking at pictures of celebrities used to inspire her. She knew that one day there would be a picture of her wearing sweatpants in a grocery store parking lot with the caption "Rachel Berry—she's just like us! She shops for groceries!" They would be designer sweatpants, though.

All of a sudden, Rachel remembered that she *was* a celebrity now! Grabbing the magazine, she ignored the cover story about how Scarlett Johansson and Ryan Reynolds might have hooked up again and flipped through it, scanning the pages.

"You gonna buy that, kid?" Mr. Grumpypants Cowboy narrowed his eyes at her. "This ain't no freebie store. Pony up."

Rachel nonchalantly tossed a twenty-dollar bill at him before walking out the double doors. "Keep the change." She thought she heard him mumble something about teenagers stealing money from their parents as she left.

Rachel sucked in her breath. There she was, wearing a plum-colored strapless cocktail dress and sky-high nude heels in the "Who Wore it Better?" section. None other than Miley Cyrus took up the other half of the page wearing the exact same thing, only with silver shoes. Rachel was the clear winner, winning by a landslide with 73 percent of the reader vote! Kurt really knew what he was doing. Rachel sipped her slushie happily as she started off back to the hotel.

In the parking lot, Rachel felt like she was being followed. "Is that Rachel Berry?" she heard someone yell. Rachel spun around and used the only weapon she had: the slushie. She threw the icy drink right into the face of a man who was quickly retreating. She craned for a better look at his face, but it was covered under a mess of curly hair. He was really dirty — now slushie-covered as well and probably homeless.

The man stumbled around in the darkness, trying to shake off the purple ice. "I knew her!" he shouted as he scampered off into the shadows. "Big star now! But... I knew her!"

Rachel shuddered and quickened her pace to get back to the hotel. That was definitely weird. Something about the whole situation gave her the creeps. She doubted the man had actually known her — he was probably just crazy and had read her name somewhere. But something about him was oddly familiar.... The curly hair, that voice. No, it couldn't be. *It's just been a long day*, she decided.

Rachel brushed the thoughts aside as she climbed back into her giant bed. She finally felt tired. If tomorrow held as many surprises as today had, Rachel Berry certainly needed all the beauty sleep she could get.

eight

Principal Figgins's office, Tuesday morning

I t's so good to have you back at McKinley, Rachel!" Principal Figgins was much more enthusiastic about her presence than Rachel had ever seen him before. Normally, when Rachel visited his office to complain about the acoustics in the choir room or came to him with suggestions of ways he could encourage the students of McKinley to practice better hygiene, he would have his secretary, Mrs. Goodrich, tell Rachel that he wasn't there—even though Rachel could see him inside, clipping his fingernails or drinking his coffee. The front of his office was made up of large glass panels, after all.

"I don't usually encourage dropouts to return and set examples for the students. But for you, I'll make an exception!" he said in his thick accent through a wide smile. "Did you know *Oklahoma!* is my favorite musical? Mrs. Figgins, too, especially loves 'The Surrey with a Fringe on Top.'" He brought his EDUCATIONAL ADMINISTRATORS ARE AWESOME mug to his lips, sipping loudly.

Kurt, who was sitting in the chair next to Rachel's, winced at the gross sound. Rather than bothering her, Principal Figgins made Rachel weirdly nostalgic for McKinley High. The welcome he'd given her, as opposed to the way he used to act around her, had Rachel looking forward to her evident reunion with her former Glee Club costars later that day.

"Well, if you and Mrs. Figgins ever visit New York City, there will be two special orchestra-section tickets with your name on them," Rachel answered, wondering if she would ever actually have to make good on that deal. She sort of hoped not. It sounded like a pain in the neck. "So, what did you have in mind for my performance at the rally?" Rachel asked, getting down to business.

For some reason, Figgins looked concerned. He looked to Kurt, who interjected, "Don't worry, Mr. Figgins. We already have it all worked out. Rachel will be singing 'Many a New Day' from her current starring role as Laurey on Broadway."

"Sounds great. Look, whatever you want to do is fine with me. As long as there is no monkey business, I am a happy man." He stood up to shake Rachel's and Kurt's hands. He did it like a politician, with both hands. Figgins had recently read an article in *Men's Health* about body language. Apparently, a two-handed shake was a "gentle power move" and showed everyone that you were in charge but still their

90

friend. As they stood, he threw in, "It's so very exciting to have *two* McKinley High alumni who have become such big stars." Rachel assumed he was talking about both her and Kurt. Principal Figgins was often a very confused person. Kurt wasn't a star; Rachel was. There were playbills with her name on them to prove it.

She was about to laugh at this silly mistake when a familiar flash of red crossed her line of vision. Rachel would know that red anywhere. *Cheerios.* But there was something she didn't expect to see. "I'm sorry — but was that Mercedes in a Cheerios uniform?" Rachel asked Figgins, who had taken out his handkerchief and begun polishing one of the many ornamental brass birds that lived in his office.

"Yes, Mercedes Jones is head Cheerio now," he said without missing a beat.

That couldn't be right. Mercedes and Kurt did have a brief stint on the Cheerios once. But, it was basically just a weird rebellious move the two of them made against Mr. Schuester. Rachel couldn't even remember why they had done it in the first place. Something about not getting enough solos? That wasn't the point, though. Coach Sylvester was awful to Mercedes, forcing her to diet and making her so weak that she almost fainted at school. Even after the whole debacle, which resulted in Mercedes's swift departure from the squad and subsequent personal protest through the consumption of Tater Tots, she said there was no way she'd ever join up again.

It just didn't make any sense that she'd be leading a huge

group of them now, wearing one of the uniforms that she'd despised so much. Rachel burst through the glass doors of the principal's office and past Mrs. Goodrich (who now beamed at her and became speechless in Rachel's presence). She ran out into the hallway, but she was pretty slow in the extremely difficult shoes Kurt had made her wear. They were black pumps with a red sole and a platform base. The red sole supposedly meant they were really special or something, but Rachel just thought they were really hard to walk in.

She finally caught up with the gaggle of red-uniformed girls with high ponytails. "Hey!" Rachel yelled. It stopped them dead in their tracks. The girls slowly parted like a red-and-black sea. Except in this instance, the part of Moses was being played by none other than Mercedes Jones. Also noticeably absent were Quinn Fabray, Brittany Pierce, and Santana Lopez — practically the holy trinity of cheerleading. At least at William McKinley High. They were probably off getting iced lattes or buying protein powder for Coach Sylvester.

Mercedes was stone-faced as she approached Rachel like a jungle cat that was about to pounce on its weak prey. "Can I help you?" she asked in a tone that was less than friendly.

"Mercedes, it's me — Rachel! I'm back for a visit!" Rachel shifted back and forth in her tall shoes. The look on Mercedes's face was starting to resemble a fire-breathing dragon.

"I know who you are. I'm not *stupid*." Mercedes still had that hip-jutting thing down. "Even though you always treated me like I was."

That was so not true. Why was Mercedes giving Rachel so much attitude? More important, though, Rachel wanted to know why Mercedes was leading a group of Cheerios around like she was in charge of them. Rachel ignored Mercedes's previous comment, deciding not to dance around the subject any longer.

"Is it true?" Rachel gestured to the WHMS top and cheerleading skirt. "Are you not only back on that terrible squad of robots, but now you're also their leader?"

"Why should it matter to you?" Mercedes shot back. "You left, Miss Thang. How's your fabulous life treating you?" It was obvious that she really didn't think Rachel's life was fabulous. Mercedes's expression was somewhere between bored and angry. She looked like she had more pressing things to do than stand here and talk to Rachel.

This was so odd. Rachel thought all her friends would be so happy to see her. Granted, she and Mercedes had butted heads from time to time in Glee Club back in the day — but this was just plain mean. Wasn't it all water under the bridge by now?

"Mercedes, don't be ridiculous," Rachel said, stepping forward to take Mercedes's hand. Maybe a softer approach would be better. "What are you doing? You hate everything the Cheerios and Coach Sylvester stand for."

Mercedes pulled away from Rachel's touch like she had poisonous skin. "Maybe I used to. But a lot has changed around here since you abandoned us like that." She lifted her arm in a grand sweeping gesture toward the pack of girls behind her. "These are my girls now. And they appreciate me a lot more than you ever did." Mercedes snapped her fingers. Heather Sims quickly shuffled up to Mercedes and handed her a bottle of water.

The whole scene started to weirdly remind Rachel of the musical *Chicago*. Mercedes looked like the character Matron "Mama" Morton with the way she was bossing around her bunch of hot teenage murderesses. Maybe the comparison was a little extreme. But at the very least, most students at McKinley High would probably agree that the Cheerios did a good job of killing everyone's self-esteem on a daily basis.

Mercedes took a sip of water and focused her attention back on Rachel. "Sorry, talking to you wore me out. Got a little thirsty. Are you done wasting my time now?"

Rachel was taken aback. She was used to Mercedes being sassy, but it was like she was a clone of Coach Sylvester now. Maybe she was just grumpy from being on that gross Cheerios diet. Coach Sylvester always made all the girls drink a concoction made with cayenne pepper, maple syrup, lemon juice, and water. Brittany had once told Rachel that it contained magical powers that made her go higher on her flips.

"Now if you'll excuse me, we have to go practice our routine for the rally." Mercedes turned to leave.

"Wait!" Rachel yelled. She had an idea. "Why don't we collaborate and perform together at the rally? I'm already doing one song on my own, but it would be great to sing with you again!" Rachel could be so brilliant.

"I really don't need you. My talents are great enough to

stand on my own, and the Cheerios appreciate that. Plus, all my fans would be really disappointed if I ruined my song by including some high-school dropout who is just trying to make herself feel better about leaving. So, thanks — but no thanks."

Kurt finally caught up to the scene. He reluctantly bowed his head toward Mercedes. "Hello," Kurt said.

Mercedes regarded him with equal disdain. "Ugh. Don't even get me started on *you*..." She appeared to be searching for the words that would do the maximum damage. "You *gator*."

Rachel had no idea what that was supposed to mean, but by the look on Kurt's face, she knew it wasn't anything positive. He was crestfallen.

Mercedes tightened her high ponytail. "Get out of my way," she snapped at Kurt before strutting off with the pretty pack of wolves.

"What's a gator?" Rachel asked as the group disappeared around the corner.

Kurt dropped his head. "A gay traitor," he answered, his voice full of sadness and shame. "We made it up during one season of *Project Runway*, when one of the contestants backstabbed his partner during judging." This was a fond memory for Kurt, and he looked wistful for a moment. "Apparently, Mercedes has become even more ruthless than Quinn ever was as captain." Kurt sighed. "At least she remembers that we used to be friends. She never liked you to begin with."

They started to stroll down the hallway. Rachel resisted

the urge to go to her locker, which was coming up on their right. "I got the scoop from Ashley Enea after you bolted from Figgins's office. After the camp—and the whole Santana thing—Mercedes went totally nuts. So when the Cheerios asked her to choreograph a hip-hop routine for nationals, she ditched Glee to help them loosen up. After they totally won all East Compton Clovers–style, she was, like, their super funk hero or something," Kurt explained.

What is this "Santana thing" that Kurt keeps mentioning? Rachel was about to ask him when the bell rang, signaling the end of a class period. All of a sudden, hundreds of students poured out into the hallway from every direction.

Because it was the last week of school, most of them were carrying copies of the new *Thunderclap* rather than textbooks. This edition had a red cover, with silver and black vertical stripes. It was completely different from the yearbook Rachel had brought to school what seemed like only a few days earlier. It was strange to think that the new one didn't contain her picture at all. It bummed her out a little. Especially because this year, her picture would have been a senior portrait—large and glossy with a quote of her choosing underneath it. She had been planning to use a Judy Garland quote: "Always be a first-rate version of yourself, instead of a second-rate version of somebody else."

A tall kid wearing a letterman's jacket bumped into her, knocking her off balance. Kurt grabbed her by the arm so she didn't topple over.

"What—are you reverting now?" he said. "Do I need to

start dressing you in horrid ballet flats again till you learn to walk like a big girl? Perhaps some neon-green Crocs?"

Rachel shuddered. Those foam atrocities should so not be allowed to exist. She might not know much about fashion, but she knew that.

"Shut up," Rachel told him, straightening her posture. "You shouldn't talk to your boss like that."

Kurt scoffed. He had been getting used to the new, nicer Rachel since they'd arrived in Lima. Guess that act was over.

Rachel watched as a tiny blond freshman girl in glasses walked up to her old locker, twisting the knob around, matching the numbers of the combination. The girl struggled with the metal slide in the exact same way Rachel used to. The locker had a tendency to stick. Suddenly, Rachel was overcome with jealousy. Watching someone else open her locker felt akin to witnessing a boyfriend cheat on her.

Almost involuntarily, Rachel ran toward the locker. "Hey — don't close that!" she yelled at the poor girl, who froze with her hand on the metal door, staring at Rachel like a deer in headlights.

"Sorry. It's just that this used to be my locker, and I kind of miss it. Would you mind letting me visit with it for a minute?" Rachel asked, aware that her bizarre question sounded more like something Brittany might say than the request of a polished Broadway star.

The girl nodded, pushing her glasses higher on her nose and looking obviously confused as she turned to leave.

"Oh, Rachel…" Kurt said, shaking his head.

Rachel caught a glimpse of red inside the locker. The girl had left her copy of the *Thunderclap* right there! Rachel couldn't help herself. She scanned the area, looking over each shoulder. Once the coast seemed clear enough, she quickly snatched the yearbook and slammed the locker door shut.

"Did you seriously just do that?" Kurt asked in disbelief. Rachel's antics never failed to appall and surprise her side-kick. "You are out of control."

"What? I'll totally put it back. I do know the combination, after all." Rachel smoothed her hands over the thick, bound *Thunderclap*. Maybe it had some of the answers she was looking for.

nine

Hallway outside choir room, Tuesday afternoon

The hallways at William McKinley High hadn't really changed much, even though Rachel's life had. It still smelled slightly like overcooked cafeteria food. Home-made posters announcing school-sponsored events still hung on the walls between the rows of tan lockers. And this week — being the very last one of the school year — the kids still buzzed with the excitement of the approaching sum-mer. They walked around the hallways sporting smiles instead of the usual frowns that took residence on their faces during the rest of the school year.

And the choir room was still in the very same spot, too. Not that Rachel had expected it to have moved or anything. But she was starting to think anything was possible after having just seen head Cheerio Mercedes in action. She stood outside the familiar door with the little glass cutout, waiting for Kurt. She resisted the urge to peek in, though. She was afraid someone would see her, and it would totally ruin the surprise.

It sounded like they were right in the middle of practice. She could hear muffled notes being played on the piano. It was probably Brad, who usually accompanied them. She had totally forgotten about him, but now that she'd thought of it, she sort of missed Brad. He always accommodated her last-minute requests and was an impeccable sight-reader. How strange. It was weird how you could miss something when you had never really given it much thought before.

Rachel tried to guess what song they were working on right now, but it was impossible to tell what it was. Whatever it was sounded off.

Rachel was getting antsy. Kurt had told her that he'd be right back, but she had absolutely no idea where he'd gone. He kept doing that. Some employee he was. Constantly ditching her to fulfill mysterious tasks elsewhere. She made a mental note to tell him he wasn't allowed do that anymore. Rachel was supposed to be the one in charge. So far, she'd felt like just a puppet. The kind with those strings on its hands. Kurt was the one who looked like Pinocchio in the ridiculous shorts-and-suspenders getup he was wearing today.

Rachel could hear Brittany's voice inside. Suddenly, all of the time she had spent in that particular room came rushing back to her. She recalled the amazing solos she'd sung. All the fights she'd fought with the other members of New Directions or Mr. Schuester. All the days she'd sat wishing she would be in the very position she was in now — a big star coming back for a visit.

She really was excited to make this surprise appearance at Glee Club practice, but the thought of seeing everyone again simultaneously made her stomach churn and her heart beat faster. It was like an audition.

But as nervous as she was, it amused Rachel that she could get so jittery over an entrance as small as this. She must have performed for hundreds (maybe even thousands) of people every night — not to mention all the red carpet events where she was probably a guest of honor. This was just a little mid-western high school.

Smoothing down her red belted shirtdress, Rachel wondered if she looked any more grown-up than she used to. The cut of the outfit was quite flattering on her and made her figure appear as if it were a little bit hourglass-shaped, as opposed to the straight-as-a-board body she actually had. And if she could manage to walk in the shoes without falling over, everyone was bound to be a little impressed with the physical transformation. She should have listened to more of Kurt's fashion advice back when they were in school. Maybe then things might have worked out between her and Finn. Just wait until he saw her today.

Rachel couldn't believe Finn kept creeping into her thoughts. Must be just the fact that she was back here. It was unavoidable. Every corner of McKinley High stirred up some old memory, and most of them involved either Finn or Glee. Or both.

She began to pace, partially because she was restless but mainly to practice walking. Falling wasn't exactly the entrance she wanted to make. Rachel had just finally begun to create her own hair-wind (another Kurt trick), when a high-pitched voice at the other end of the hallway startled her.

"Do my eyes deceive me?" it squealed in disbelief.

A short, bespectacled nerd with an unmistakable mess of curly hair excitedly shuffled toward her. It was none other than J-Fro, the school's resident gossip and number-one Rachel Berry fan. His crush on Rachel had always bordered on unhealthy obsession, but his presence made Rachel feel like she should have been experiencing a little more of this adoration from her former classmates now that she was back in town.

As J-Fro got closer, Rachel thought she could see little streams of tears rolling down his cheeks. "Are you...crying?" Rachel had seen old footage of Beatles fans crying hysterically when they would catch a glimpse of Ringo Starr or Paul McCartney.

"Is it really you? My goddess—*the* Rachel Berry?" J-Fro began panting like a dog. "Has the queen of McKinley finally returned to the kingdom to reclaim her rightful throne of epic hotness?" he said in all seriousness, dabbing his eyes with a dirty hanky. "I have waited for so long for this day to come." J-Fro pulled out his cell phone and began snapping pictures, a mere three inches from Rachel's face.

"Jacob!" Rachel held up her right hand in protest. "What did I tell you about doing that?"

"Oh, sorry, I forgot your four-inch personal-space rule." He wiped a large glob of drool from the corner of his mouth. He took a step backward, panting.

"No, the other rule." Rachel tossed her hair over her shoulder and struck a pose. "About only getting shots of my good side." This was something she had discovered through many hours of posing in her bedroom mirror, as well as taking pictures on her webcam. Her right side was definitely better. She smiled wide.

"Sweet heavens," J-Fro said as he frantically searched his backpack. He located a larger camera and popped off the lens cap. He began snapping away, a camera in each hand. "I'm so glad I visited that witch doctor and had him bring you back to me again. Never leave." His body was practically vibrating with excitement.

Now this was more like it. Rachel kissed the palm of her hand and blew it toward J-Fro's cameras. Across the hall, Puck leaned against the lockers, watching the whole scene play out. Rachel had been focusing so hard on sucking in her cheekbones that she hadn't even noticed him there. He caught her attention when he casually put his hand up to "catch" her kiss and pretended to put it in a front pocket of his dark-wash jeans. Ah, good old Puck. The devious smirk. The sexy swagger. It looked like he still had that bad-boy-charm thing down. And it looked like he was checking her out.

Rachel and Puck had a weird romantic history. It mostly consisted of using each other from time to time to get back at others. Or rather, Rachel had just used him to make Finn jealous. And Puck couldn't really help himself if presented with the opportunity to make out with a hot chick. He'd pretty much already hooked up with every single girl in Glee Club, maybe the whole school. Even Lauren Zizes. He had pissed a lot of them off, too. That much was evident by how often the fights that broke out in the girls' bathroom at lunch could be traced back to one name: Puck.

"Don't hate the Puckster—hate the game" was usually his response when asked what he had to say for himself. At least he was honest.

Puck took out his own cell and snapped a few candid shots of Rachel. *Wow*, Rachel thought. *Even Puck is one of my fans now.* He winked at her before continuing his stroll down the hallway to who knows where. Wait—where *was* he going? Shouldn't he be in Glee practice with the others right now?

"Puck! Wait!" He spun around to face her.

"Oooh, yes. Hold that face, it's working for me. That sort of surprised-worried-shy look. Oh, yes." J-Fro's eyes fluttered, and he began to emit a noise that frightened Rachel. Maybe that was enough pictures for now.

Rachel ran up to Puck. "It's so good to look at you—I mean, see you."

A slow smile spread over his tanned face. He'd probably already started his summer ritual of working as a pool boy to the local cougars. Puck didn't discriminate against older women.

"You, too, sweet cheeks. There's no one nearly as annoying around here anymore. I sorta missed you bossing me around...." He patted her on the shoulder.

Puck looked kind of different. Maybe it was just weird to look at everything from so much higher up in these crazy shoes. It felt like she was practically looking him in the eye. Or at least not looking up his nose like before. Rachel had seen up a lot of noses in her time. It was one of the disadvantages of being the size of a Smurf. There were many advantages of it, though, like being comfortable in coach on flights. Not that she had to worry about that anymore.

"Why aren't you in Glee practice? It's going on in there right now." Rachel motioned to the door. She ignored J-Fro whimpering helplessly in the background. Rachel's eyes narrowed. "You didn't quit or something, did you?" That would be so like him to just up and leave the minute she wasn't there to hold the club together anymore. He'd probably taken up pro wrestling or started an escort service since she'd seen him last.

Puck didn't miss a beat. "Look, hot stuff—I'd love to, but I can't stay and chat. I've got things to see and people to *do*."

What a pig, Rachel thought.

And with that, Puck rushed off. Why did everyone keep doing that? Puck was definitely up to no good. *At least some things don't change*, Rachel thought as visions of the new, scary Mercedes flashed through her mind.

"If you are quite finished with your little nostalgic flirting session, may I suggest we go inside before practice is over? Or are we trying to build suspense?" Kurt crossed his arms over his purple shirt and cocked his eyebrow at her. Rachel hadn't even seen him come back.

Of course she was ready. She was the one who had been waiting for him in the first place! "Lead the way, Hummel," Rachel said as she combed her fingers through her hair. This was it. The big entrance.

She briefly considered going in with a song, like that time at regionals. She'd entered through the back of the auditorium singing "Don't Rain on My Parade." But she didn't have anything good prepared at the present moment. Better stick with a plain old grand entrance.

Kurt took a deep breath and pushed the door open. They stepped through together.

"Oh, hey, guys," Brittany said casually, as if not a single day had gone by since she'd last seen the two of them. "Are you guys, like, rejoining Glee Club? You're late for practice, but it's okay."

Rachel just stared blankly at her. She was too shocked by what she saw in front of her to respond.

Rather than a room full of familiar faces (that were overjoyed to see her), she and Kurt were greeted by the sight of about a dozen prepubescent strangers. Brittany stood at the head of the classroom, sans Cheerios uniform, waving her arms around like a cartoon conductor. She was wearing a really short denim skirt and a camisole that revealed even more than her uniform used to.

The kids — who must have been freshmen — looked like they were the runtiest, geekiest picks of the new litter. They wore expressions that ranged from wonder to complete terror. A small blond girl in the back looked like a scared rodent. She bit her nails nervously. However, the most peculiar part was what they were all wearing. Each kid was sporting a red cone-shaped party hat.

It reminded Rachel of her sixth birthday party. It was the year that her dads had invited a bunch of kids from her kindergarten class to their house. They'd made pretty invitations that said A STAR IS BORN below a picture of Judy Garland. She had recently seen the movie and had become obsessed with it. Rachel was so excited for the big day. Sadly, not a single kid ended up coming to the party. She had never really been popular, even then. Probably because Rachel was always trying to upstage everyone during circle time. She'd hit her first F note while singing the alphabet song, even though it wasn't part of the tune. She liked to improvise.

In an attempt to save the shindig, Rachel's dads invited over all their community-theater friends and coworkers instead. It ended up being a huge group of adults, all sitting around drinking wine and wearing children's party hats. Then they all watched the movie together. Six-year-old Rachel performed "The Man That Got Away" to a standing ovation in the living room. She'd thought it was the best birthday ever.

With the exception of the hats, this was nothing like that.

A skinny redheaded boy in green suspenders bumped into Rachel carelessly as he began passing out what appeared to be fake white beards to the rest of the kids. Rachel wanted to ask why on earth they were dressing like Santa Claus in the middle of June (everyone knew how much Brittany loved the guy), but she couldn't even speak. There was no way this was Glee Club.

Kurt was able to form a sentence first. "Britt, where is everyone?" He stood frozen, his mouth agape.

Brittany looked around the room, surveying the motley crew that was present. She was like Little Bo Peep presiding over her little flock (right before she lost them and everything).

Brittany was majorly confused. "We're totally all here. Even cardboard Bieber." She pointed to the back row, and sure enough, a life-size cutout of Justin Bieber stood, also wearing a red party hat.

"You can't be serious! Brittany, think. Who is missing?" Rachel gasped for air. This couldn't be happening. She didn't know any of these people. There was no Tina, Artie, or Sam present. No Mike Chang. No Finn. And worst of all, no Mr. Schuester. What was the world coming to?

"Oh, do you mean Jessica? I forgot she told me she couldn't come anymore because she has to run her hamster day-care center," Brittany said in her vacant, calm voice. A few of the kids groaned. Jessica must have been a big asset to the club. But that was beside the point.

"Are you...in charge here?" Kurt squeaked. He looked shaken for the first time today.

"Are rainbows made of Skittles?" Brittany giggled. "Duh, of course! You guys are totally lucky that you came back on Gnome Day, too. I have extra hats and beards." The red-headed kid held out a few sets of the strange accessories to Rachel and Kurt. They didn't take them.

Brittany then pulled out a tub of Vaseline and started passing it around to the group. Each student took a little bit from the container and rubbed it onto their elbows before passing it along. "You guys want some?" she said to Rachel and Kurt, who stood nearby, still in a state of complete shock.

"What...is...that?" Kurt asked, still horrified by the turn of events.

"It's elbow grease. My dad said it helps when you are try-ing to work on something. I always make my club use it. We get so much further with a little bit of it." She smiled and nodded knowingly.

"That's...so not right." Kurt grabbed Brittany's arm and pulled her to the side of the room. She winced in pain. "We need to talk to you."

Rachel felt weird with all these little freshmen staring at her with their beady eyes. "Um, go back to practicing," she said to the group, secretly wondering if they were any good.

A few moments later, they began singing "Ain't No Moun-tain High Enough" by Marvin Gaye and Tammi Terrell, only the words were a little off. It sounded like the group had replaced every *no* in the song with the word *gnome*. Is that what Brittany had meant by *Gnome Day*? Rachel shook her head in defeat.

"Where is Mr. Schuester?" Rachel demanded, kicking her shoes off her feet. There was no point in making a good impression now. This room was full of losers. Rachel's toes throbbed.

"Oh, he left." Brittany shrugged. "He found a baby unicorn when he was hiking and captured it. I think he's touring the world, showing it in all its magical glory." Brittany always spoke in an awed, hushed tone. "I hope I get to see it." She was completely serious.

Clearly, information from Brittany wasn't ever that reliable. Mr. Schuester was gone, though. They just had to figure out why.

"When did he leave? Did he say when the 'unicorn tour' was stopping back in Ohio?" Kurt asked, trying a different approach.

Brittany shook her head. "No, but I decided to run New Directions myself until he gets back. These are all the new members I've recruited from the youth music camp! Aren't they mini?" Brittany looked very pleased with herself. She loved "things that were the wrong size" and often could be seen carrying around doll shoes or a giant ear of corn. Nobody really questioned it.

"You totally should have been a counselor with us last summer. It was so much fun. And now they are all in Glee!" Brittany lowered her voice. "I've even hooked up with one of them. One special guy..."

Rachel looked back at the group of dancing gnomes. Brittany was known for hooking up with whoever happened to be nearby whenever the urge hit. But they all looked so... young.

"Are you serious?" Rachel asked in minor disbelief.

Brittany giggled. "Shhh! He's looking at us right now." Brittany gave a flirtatious wave to the Justin Bieber standee in the back row. Her blond hair fell around her face coquettishly. "He *gets* me."

"Well, Brittany. I'm glad you finally found a man you can hold a conversation with. I'm sure you and cardboard Bieber will be very happy together. Just don't go swimming." Kurt patted her on the shoulder. He knew that they weren't going to get much more information out of her. He decided it was better to just watch the train wreck in fascination.

"Thanks, Kurt. That means a lot. I have to get back to my club now. They really need me."

They had, indeed, stopped singing. *Thank God for that*, Rachel thought.

Brittany skipped back to the head of the room. "Okay everyone, let's move on to 'Bad Gnomance.' You ready?" Apparently, she still had some of that old Cheerios-style pep in her. The looks of admiration on their faces implied that the kids in Brittany's weird Glee Club would do almost anything for her. "Yes, Queen B," they all said in unison. It was like some bizarre cult.

"And-uh one, and-uh two, and-uh three!" Brittany shouted, dancing around, not realizing that she had just flashed half the room by doing a high kick in her miniskirt. All the boys' eyes bugged out. Maybe that was the key to her success.

Rachel sighed heavily. It didn't matter what the reason was. Glee Club had completely fallen apart since they'd left. Not only was Mr. Schuester missing, but everything he had worked so hard to build in the last few years was just gone. It was really sad.

"Come on, Kurt. Let's go." Rachel picked up her shoes and padded out into the hallway barefoot. She couldn't bear to watch "practice" any longer. It was official: McKinley High had gone totally insane without Rachel Berry. Now she just had to find Mr. Schuester and get to the bottom of things. Maybe there was more to the story. Until then, it wouldn't hurt to see Finn, either. After a day like today, he was just what she needed.

ten

McKinley High gymnasium, later Tuesday afternoon

The McKinley High School gym looked the same as it always had. Rows of worn bleachers were pulled out from the wall lining the basketball court. Handmade posters of various colors and sizes hung on the walls, bearing slogans meant to cheer on the mediocre teams. Sports had never been McKinley's strong point. The Titans hardly ever won anything until Coach Beiste came along, replacing a heartbroken Coach Tanaka (whose personal life affected his coaching skills a little too much) last season. The baseball team still needed work. Lots of it.

Still, and maybe it was to the credit of the award-winning Cheerios, McKinley High had tons of spirit. This much was evident by the group of students who now stood in the middle of the court, unpacking the traditional end-of-year rally decorations. They began unfurling a bunch of red and white streamers that looked as if they'd been reused for a decade. Rachel wouldn't be surprised if they actually had. Most of the budget for extracurricular activities was usually funneled straight to the Cheerios. Coach Sylvester had always made sure of that.

In an effort to have a few moments to herself, Rachel was sitting at the top of the bleachers. She used to sit here and watch Finn during basketball practice. The hard bench was uncomfortable, but it had suddenly become necessary to hide out from the crowds of students. Word had spread throughout the school that the Broadway star Rachel Berry had returned from the big city. It turned out that she actually had plenty of fans. Granted, most of them were kids who hadn't known her at all during her days at McKinley. Back then, they had either chosen to ignore her completely or didn't know she existed. The rest were freshmen who had heard stories of Rachel making her own way to fame and fortune. Either way, it felt pretty good to have fans.

Whenever she walked by clusters of students, Rachel would hear whispers of admiration, sprinkled with the sound of camera phones snapping pictures. It seemed as if everyone wanted to get a shot of the famous Miss Berry. As of now, she was definitely a trending topic on Twitter in the Lima area, if not the whole state of Ohio.

Rachel enjoyed all the attention from the McKinley paparazzi. But it was a little strange how some of the kids were taking pictures of her from such weird angles. One of the junior varsity football players, Jake Lader, had even propped up a ladder by the trophy case. He'd pretended to be polishing the Cheerios championship statues. When Rachel had walked by, he'd quickly snapped some photos from above. She'd be surprised if those shots contained little else than a view down her shirt. What good were those, anyway? Her face was the real moneymaker.

Rachel unearthed the stolen copy of the *Thunderclap* from her designer handbag. Now that she was alone, she could explore it without Kurt looking over her shoulder. To be honest, she was getting a little sick of his snide comments about everything.

That very morning, he'd chided Rachel about her poor posture. Not only was that ridiculous (Rachel had always prided herself on having perfect posture), but it was also bitchy. When she'd told him to keep it to himself, he just snorted and went back to criticizing her. Rachel was beginning to get the feeling that her closest employee did not enjoy working for her. Unfathomable.

She'd already been in Lima for more than twenty-four hours, but Rachel wasn't any closer to figuring out what had happened to Mr. Schuester. No one seemed to know anything regarding his whereabouts. The closest she'd gotten to any real information was from Kelly Mahoney. Rachel had accosted her when she'd overheard Kelly mention his name to Spencer Richards by the library.

"Excuse me, but did I just hear you mention Mr. Schuester?" Rachel interrupted. Kelly was not a Rachel Berry fan. It had to do with some incident last year where Rachel had supposedly cut in front of her in line during lunch, saying that she was more important to the school and therefore had authority to do so.

It turned out that Kelly had heard that Mr. Schuester had also gone to New York. That certainly made more sense than Brittany's unicorn story, but it still seemed unlikely.

Rachel began to flip through the pages of the yearbook, searching for the foreign language section. If Mr. Schuester would appear anywhere, it would be there. Even though running Glee Club had been his real passion, his main occupation had been teaching Spanish at McKinley.

She shifted uncomfortably, trying to get the backs of her thighs to stop sticking to the bench. It was really hot inside the gym, and Rachel felt herself starting to sweat. She should probably get going soon. No one liked a smelly star.

She continued to scan the pages until a commotion down below caught her attention. Coach Sue Sylvester had barged in and started ruthlessly criticizing the lackluster rally decorations.

"You call these decorations? My handicapable sister could do better than this with some toilet paper and a chain saw. I don't want my Cheerios performing beneath something that makes my eyes bleed." Coach Sylvester ripped down a dangling red streamer as she stormed out the gym doors. "Fix it!"

Coach Sylvester was just as awful as ever. Rachel had

always thought that her attitude was because of her ongoing bitter rivalry with Mr. Schuester and Glee Club. She was the one who would always try to get him fired and New Directions disbanded. Apparently, she was just a miserable person.

Wait a second—Coach Sylvester *was* always the one trying to get rid of Mr. Schuester! If he was gone, it was almost guaranteed that she had something to do with it. Rachel slammed the yearbook shut, shoved it in her bag, and stumbled down the steps. She had to catch up with her and demand some answers.

Thankfully, it was much easier to get around in the outfit Kurt had dressed her in this afternoon. He had chosen a menswear-inspired look that was very *Annie Hall*—a gray pinstripe vest and tie with a khaki miniskirt and black oxford shoes. It looked sort of mannish. It was probably inspired by Kurt's motto, "Fashion has no gender." Admittedly, the shoes were an odd choice for summertime, but at least Rachel could walk.

She ran out of the gym after Coach Sylvester, who was powering through the hallways like there was a last-minute sale on her favorite appletini-flavored protein powder.

"Coach Sylvester!" Rachel hollered at the tracksuit-clad figure. "I need to talk to you!" It was a losing battle. Either Coach Sylvester was completely ignoring all of Rachel's attempts to garner her attention on purpose, or she'd developed terrible hearing in the past year.

Rachel gave up. It wasn't worth chasing after her like

some desperate girl who'd just been cut from the cheerleading squad. Rachel Berry didn't follow. She led.

She figured it was time to find Kurt to see what was next on the agenda. He'd planned a packed week for Rachel that even included some appearances on local television. Also, Rachel decided she should probably brush up on her routine for the rally. The press was going to be there to broadcast the whole thing. Undoubtedly, there would also be several amateur recordings posted on YouTube by students the next day.

One had to be in top form at all times. The Internet was a brutal place. Rachel had learned that the hard way with her MySpace page. The constant negative comments from various members of the Cheerios were very hurtful. There would be none of that this time around.

Rachel straightened her tie and tried to decide her next move. If you were Kurt, where would you go?

"Rachel, is that you?" Artie Abrams wheeled his chair up to her. He was dressed head to toe in black. It looked like he'd inked a Jolly Roger skull and crossbones on his backpack with Wite-Out. How odd. Since when was Artie Goth? "I'd heard that you were back. . . . I just didn't believe it. You look great." There was sadness in his voice.

"Thanks, Artie. . . . So do you." Rachel may have been a professional actress, but it didn't sound too convincing once the words had left her mouth. In truth, he looked like a mess. Artie was normally clean-cut, favoring sweater-vests and shampoo. She didn't get close enough to find out, but she was pretty sure he smelled bad.

Artie gestured at his outfit. "Oh, you don't have to lie. I know I look bad. This is just part of the latest scheme I've cooked up." Artie began to crack his knuckles, which was a nervous habit. His hands often seized up from wheeling himself around, even with the special fingerless leather gloves he wore.

"Scheme? What exactly are you trying to accomplish — being the smelliest McKinley student?" Rachel blurted out. Once again, she felt bad for being so harsh. He did look bummed. "Though I could probably compete with you for that title right now," she quickly added. She *had* gotten really sweaty while sitting in the gym.

He finally cracked a smile. "No, you couldn't. You're not a McKinley student anymore, remember?" Artie was always such a nice guy. It was strange that she hadn't thought of what had become of him at all.

"No, I suppose I'm not. Isn't it weird how everything worked out?" Rachel awkwardly joked.

"If by weird, you mean terrible, then yes." Artie was stone-faced. "You abandoned us, Rachel. I hate to say it, but you were some sort of crazy glue for Glee Club. As soon as you said no to helping us last summer, everything just fell apart." His jaw tightened. "You want to know why I'm dressed like this? It's because I have no other way to get Tina to notice me." He slumped down in his chair.

Rachel actually began to feel really bad. But she still didn't see how it was her fault. New Directions had always been sort of fragile and just waiting to crumble at the slightest setback. "I'm sorry, but what does my leaving have to do with you and Tina?" It was a valid question.

"Weren't you the one who said that being a part of something special is what makes you special?" Artie took off his gloves and began wringing his hands. "That's what Glee was for me. Everyone else went off and became great at other things. This was all I had." He still hadn't really answered Rachel's question. "Now I'm just left trying to win back my first true love with silly tactics like this instead of songs." Artie motioned to his black ensemble.

It was hard for Rachel to believe that any girl would swoon for his current look. Even Tina, who rocked a much better version of the style he was going for. Boys were so weird sometimes.

"Oh." Rachel hadn't considered that Glee Club was just as important to someone else as it had been to her. "Why didn't you stay in Brittany's Glee Club?" She couldn't think of any other solution.

"Do you really want me to answer that?" Artie now looked at her like *she* was the crazy one. "They'd probably dress me up as a roller skate and use me as one of Brittany's giant props."

He had a point. Rachel had a feeling that Artie wasn't completely over Brittany, either. The two of them had dated last year when Glee Club was at the peak of its popularity. It wasn't a very high peak. Rachel looked down at Artie. Were those tears forming in his eyes? *Oh no.* She hoped not — she wouldn't know how to handle that. Tears of joy at the sight of her were okay; tears of any other kind...not so much. Artie sniffled but managed to hold it together.

"What are you even doing here right now?" Rachel asked, starting to wonder the same thing about herself.

Artie rolled back and forth, which was totally the wheelchair equivalent of nervous pacing. "I'm waiting." Rachel raised her eyebrows at him. "For Tina to get out of her AP art final. She has to paint a self-portrait while Ms. Kowalski watches."

"Artie! You can't just sit around and stalk her. For people who aren't celebrities like me, that really freaks them out. Anyway, isn't she still with Mike Chang?" Rachel was actually surprised that she'd remembered this little detail about someone else's life. See? She wasn't totally selfish.

"Yeah, but a guy can dream, right?"

He really was pathetic. Rachel had never seen him so dejected. Maybe Glee Club had really made a difference in his confidence level. After all, not everyone possessed Rachel's natural charisma and high self-esteem. She was trying to think of something else to say that could possibly comfort him when Finn and Quinn came strolling down the hall.

It was like a flashback to sophomore year. Everything seemed to move in slow motion. They were holding hands, and Quinn had that smug look on her face like she owned the whole world. Rachel knew it well, though that look normally accompanied a Cheerios uniform, which was almost the same as owning the world — at least at McKinley High.

But today Quinn was wearing a simple blue dress. It may have been plain, but it looked expensive. It seemed as if Quinn Fabray was still her family's little princess, even after the whole teen-pregnancy thing. Around her neck was her trademark diamond cross necklace. She had that whole virginal innocence thing down. Which was ironic, given the circumstances.

Finn didn't look that different, either. Except maybe more tan. He was wearing his favorite dark gray T-shirt (the one Rachel used to love snuggling up to because it was so soft) and his adorable crooked smile. His chocolate-colored hair was at the perfect length — he'd probably gotten it cut about three weeks ago. Not too short, not too long. Rachel's heart thumped in her chest. How did the sight of Finn still manage to do that to her?

Finn leaned down and kissed Quinn on the forehead. The forehead? That was the sweetest spot to kiss anyone, Rachel had always thought. Whenever Finn kissed her there, she had felt so loved and safe. In truth, he was so tall (and she was so short) that it was just easier to kiss her there if they were standing up. But still. That was *her* spot! The nerve!

"Not so easy to get over someone, is it?" Artie said, snapping Rachel out of her current state. "Yeah, I bet you never thought that they would get back together, huh?"

There was no way she was admitting to still being in love

with Finn—but she wanted to know more. "Well, no, but they, um, look happy. How long has this been going on for?"

Artie smirked at her. He was no fool. "Quite a while."

What a vague answer! That could be any length of time. Rachel had to know how long Finn had waited after she'd left before he started dating around again. Had she meant nothing to him? There should have been at least an eight-month-long grief period from the moment she left Lima. It would take at least that long for her star presence to wear off. Maybe more.

"Honestly, they started hooking up again during the youth music camp last summer. Something about realizing that they never gave their relationship a real chance after all that baby drama." Artie shrugged nonchalantly. "I'm pretty sure that once you were finally out of the picture, there were no distractions left keeping them from trying it out again. And having all those adorable children around to take care of helped. It was like they were playing house or something." Artie paused, then added, "It was kinda gross watching them, actually. They are, like, the perfect couple now."

They did look like something out of the L.L.Bean catalog. Quinn dropped something on the ground, and Finn bent down to get it for her. While he was kneeling, he took the opportunity to kiss her hand as if she were a medieval maiden. She blushed and pulled him back up to her, giggling. Rachel felt sick.

Back to business. "But why did they quit Glee? I thought they enjoyed performing...." said Rachel. Just because you had hooked up with someone didn't mean you had to give up singing. That would be a total deal breaker. And Quinn was obviously no longer head Cheerio.

"They didn't have time for it anymore once they restarted the Celibacy Club." Artie looked bored with this conversation now. He would much rather be talking about how to solve his own problems or playing video games. "They've become really involved in Quinn's church, and they're the poster children for abstinence education."

Rachel snorted. "Miss Teen Pregnancy and Mr. Afternoon Delight?" Rachel still wasn't over the time Finn had lied to her about sleeping with Santana in some gross motel. Not a classy move. And the two of them running an abstinence club could not be more hypocritical.

Finn finally drew his adoring gaze away from Quinn long enough to notice Rachel and Artie. "Hey, Artie! Hey, Rachel! Good to see you!" he yelled, sounding like he actually meant it. Finn lifted his arm to wave at them. But what she saw next nearly made Rachel pass out.

Finn's forearm was covered in a gigantic, elaborate cross tattoo. Beneath it was another sizable design that said *Quinn* in loopy letters. *Oh no!* Even putting aside the fact that he had declared his love for Rachel's former nemesis on his body, Rachel was not a big fan of body ink. She'd always thought one must remain completely malleable for the starring roles of his or her future. It was important to remain entirely free of body art or piercings (except maybe one hole in each earlobe). How would Finn's giant cross look if he were starring as Fiyero in *Wicked?* It would probably require more makeup than Elphaba's whole green look. Tattoos were so permanent and pedestrian.

By the looks of it, though, Finn wasn't headed toward a Broadway career like Rachel was. At best, he didn't look like he was headed anywhere farther than Lima Community College and a job at Burt Hummel's auto shop. Such a waste of hotness and talent. At least he looked happy.

Quinn didn't even bother to glance in Rachel's direction. She was far too entranced by the hunky man in front of her to tear her eyes away for a second. Finn leaned down to kiss Quinn, then picked up Quinn's purse so she didn't have to carry it herself.

Rachel felt her bottom lip start to quiver. This was not at all how she'd imagined her reunion with Finn.

"Sorry, dude. Now you know how I feel," Artie offered before rolling off to spy on Tina through the door of the art room.

All of a sudden, Rachel understood the adage "It's lonely at the top." Even after everything she'd accomplished—a starring role on Broadway, a personal staff, and a private jet— what did she really have to show for it? Absent parents and a broken heart. She didn't even have a high school diploma. *Maybe you can't actually plan everything,* Rachel thought.

She began to search for Kurt. She was tired of being alone. She hoped he could offer her some companionship or at least a new outfit. Some shoes that made her feel taller again. Because Rachel Berry suddenly felt very, very small.

eleven

Lima TV news station, Wednesday morning

Just remember — you're here to promote *Oklahoma!* and the McKinley performance, okay? Try not to talk too much about yourself." Kurt was busy prompting Rachel for the seventh time that morning. The two of them sat in the back of the same old, smelly limousine, speeding through the downtown area toward the local news station. Kurt had set up a promotional interview to garner more attention for Thursday's rally. If someone had been living under a rock the past few days and didn't know that Rachel was in town — they would after this.

"Last time, when you went off on that tangent with Margo Rose Ferderer about why you knew you were going to win a Tony, it took me days to do damage control. Your ego really knows no bounds sometimes."

Rachel wasn't really listening to him. "Sure...yeah," she answered while staring out the window.

Although it was early, it already looked like it was getting hot outside. People on the streets strolled by in shorts and tank tops, just going about their day. They were oblivious to the fact that the only thing that separated them from a major star was a tinted window and a car door. Rachel wondered whether they'd even care.

So far, being a star hadn't been as satisfying as she'd hoped. The best part had to be performing onstage, like she'd always wanted to. Rachel still couldn't figure out why she had no recollection of being on Broadway. The shock of being back home again after all this time was to blame. That had to be it.

Rachel sipped the hazelnut iced coffee in her hand. It tasted gross. Bitter with a sickeningly sweet aroma. But according to Kurt, it was her favorite. She never really liked coffee before. It certainly had a kick to it, but Rachel had never needed to rely on stimulants to be hyperactive. She just naturally buzzed with excitement and enthusiasm. She was beginning to feel like she didn't even know herself anymore. It wasn't a good feeling.

"Am I going to be singing on-air?" Rachel hadn't warmed up her vocal cords at all. Maybe there would be time once they arrived at the studio.

Kurt fluffed the air around Rachel's face. "No, but knowing you—you could break out in song at any moment." Kurt licked his finger and tried to wipe some dirt from Rachel's face.

"Kurt! Is this what you were doing when I threw that coconut at your head? Because you are *so* crossing a line right now." He was like a terrible stage mother. "Don't make me do it again."

Kurt grumbled something under his breath. Whatever it was, Rachel knew it wasn't complimentary. Well, that was fine. He could be upset. Rachel didn't really feel like coddling him about it. She had much heavier things on her mind.

The past day had really shaken her up. With the news about Glee Club's demise, seeing pitiful Artie, and—the painful cherry on top—Finn and Quinn being so in love, Rachel was feeling pretty terrible.

The limousine pulled into the parking lot of the station. Tall broadcast satellite dishes extended from the top of the building. A bright blue sign that read WOHN-TV hung on the brick exterior. News vans outfitted with the same logo and similar equipment lined the front. At the end of the row, however, was a pretty rare sight.

There weren't many 1979 Renault Le Cars driving around in Lima, or anywhere for that matter. It definitely belonged to Sue Sylvester. She had bought the car for this very reason— she always wanted to be special. It was one of the many items she considered her pride and joy (along with her prized tracksuit collection and rooms full of cheerleading trophies).

Coach Sylvester had royally flipped out last year when Mercedes filled the Renault's tailpipe with Tater Tots in protest. She had been instrumental in banning the snack from the McKinley High cafeteria, and Mercedes hadn't taken the news lightly.

At the time, Rachel thought it was pretty funny, but she quickly grew tired of hearing Coach Sylvester complain about the "lingering stench of Tots" and the "destruction of society through today's idiotic youth." She was also pretty sure that Coach Sylvester had taken it out on her Cheerios, whom she made do twice as many practices to "save them from their own impulses." Coach Sylvester wasn't a fan of radical ideas. Unless they were her own.

Which was precisely the reason why Coach Sylvester's Le Car was parked in front of Lima's local news station. The coach had her own weekly segment called "Sue's Corner." It covered a range of topics, but it mostly ended up being an offensive rant each week. It was the highest-rated segment of the entire news show. Week after week, Lima would tune in to find out exactly "how Sue 'Cs' it." It hadn't crossed Rachel's mind until now that she might run into the devil in a red tracksuit.

"Am I appearing on 'Sue's Corner'?" Rachel whipped around to face Kurt. He replied with a noncommittal shrug. This confirmed her worst fear. Coach Sylvester was going to eat her alive on live television.

A few minutes later, Rachel found herself being led to a humble dressing room. There was a mirror bordered by lightbulbs so she could touch up her makeup and get ready to go on camera. There was also a plastic chair and a trash can. So it wasn't exactly the *Today* show. Good thing Rachel couldn't even remember what the greenroom there had looked like. She only knew that she had been there because Kurt told her that, just a few weeks earlier, she'd been interviewed by Matt Lauer. She kept forgetting to look it up online.

"Thank you very much," Rachel told the production assistant who'd shown her to the room. He didn't look at all thrilled to be in her presence. He wore a beard, a headset, and an unwelcoming, grumpy expression. He'd probably had dreams of becoming a filmmaker someday but had never made it out of Lima. At least Rachel had gotten out. Right?

"There's a mirror there," he said, and slammed the door unceremoniously. Was that a hint?

She turned and stared at her reflection in the grungy mirror. Her hair fell perfectly around her face, thanks to Kurt's tireless efforts. She wore a conservative yet sexy blue top that made her appear to be ample-chested. How did Kurt manage to do it? He was definitely earning whatever she was paying him, even if he was a pain in the neck.

Rachel began to study her face. She didn't *look* much happier than the bearded guy. There was a dead look in her eyes, too. She really needed to snap out of it. It was showtime!

Kurt peeked in. "Do you need anything before you go on?" He was sucking up now. Good.

"Yes, another one of those iced coffees, please," Rachel said. She searched in her leather bag for something to really make her mouth stand out.

131

"Right away, Miss Berry. On in fifteen." Kurt flitted off to fulfill her wishes.

After reapplying her red lipstick, Rachel watched herself in the mirror as she sang some warm-up scales. It felt good to do vocal exercises again. So calming. She was halfway through her third set of arpeggios starting from middle C when Coach Sylvester appeared out of nowhere. She stood behind Rachel, and they locked eyes in the reflection of the mirror. "Hey there, Berry Pop-Tart. That was some real pretty singing." She put her hand on Rachel's right shoulder. It was one of Coach Sylvester's power moves. She liked to feel her prey squirm before ripping it to shreds.

Rachel nodded curtly. "Hello, Coach Sylvester."

A slow, creepy smile spread across Coach Sylvester's face. "So glad you decided to join me on my humble little slice of the media pie, *muchacha.* You ready to get thrown to the wolves?" Coach Sylvester chuckled at her own joke, then interrupted her own laughter before Rachel had any time to react. "I'm only kidding, of course. I'm actually very happy to have you as my guest on today's edition of 'Sue's Corner.'" She tightened her grip on Rachel's shoulder. "You know why that is, Bat Mitzvah Barbie?"

Rachel shook her head, but she didn't take her eyes off Coach Sylvester's. The coach had the freaky ability to seem both nice and terrifying at the same time, and it made Rachel uneasy. The wheels inside Coach Sylvester's head were spinning so fast that Rachel could practically hear them. "I can see you are at a loss for words, so I'll just go ahead and tell ya,

Princess." Coach Sylvester had begun to pace the room, gesturing wildly for effect as she delivered the blow.

"You are perfect for today's topic because you are an expert in it! It's all about achieving your dreams — no matter how many lives you ruin to do it. You, Miss Sassypants, pretty much wrote the book on that." The yellow color of Coach Sylvester's tracksuit today matched her blond hair, making her look like a giant tube of mustard. Rachel hated mustard with a passion. Coach Sylvester didn't rank much higher.

"Excuse me?" Rachel's words were so full of contempt that she didn't feel it necessary to say more than that. Anyone would get the hint.

"Aw, you should be proud of yourself! I always knew you were unbearably annoying, but I never thought you had it in you to be so *ruthless*. Yowza!" Coach Sylvester clapped her hands together excitedly. "Leaving your precious Glee Club behind like that when you were so obviously their greatest asset? You remind me of a young Sue Sylvester, Rachel. You do well today and maybe I'll even take you on as my co-anchor. We'll call you Tweety. I've always thought you looked like a ridiculously small cartoon bird." Coach Sylvester winked at her before slamming the door.

What in the world was going on? Rachel wasn't an awful person — she'd just followed her dreams. It was unfair of Coach Sylvester to assume the worst in her just because she lived her own life that way. Rachel Berry was better than that.

Even though her impulse was to up and leave, Rachel was a professional. She couldn't just ditch an interview. However, she might be able to use this appearance to her advantage. Maybe, just maybe, she could twist Coach Sylvester's wicked agenda into something that might portray her in a better light. She could even publicly apologize to all her friends and make them love her again. It was really starting to grate on her that the people she actually cared about at McKinley were upset with her. The throngs of adoring fans were great — but weirdly enough, her heart ached to have the old gang back together, all of them rolling their eyes at one of her ludicrous ideas. The good old days. Maybe she had jumped ship too early.

There was a soft knock on the door. "Come in!" Rachel yelled. She was getting fired up now. Kurt entered with her iced coffee.

"Almost ready?" he asked her gently, afraid of the crazed look in her eyes. She grabbed the cup from his hand and chugged it. Kurt watched in awe as she dabbed her red lips with a napkin. Rachel had become possessed. It wasn't the first time he'd ever seen her like this, but it was frightening nonetheless.

"Let's go." Rachel ran her fingers through her hair and stepped out into the bustling studio. There were large cameras on rolling tripods everywhere. A huge sign above them said ON AIR and would presumably light up once the show went live.

A sound guy came up and started to attach a wireless

lavalier microphone to her shirt. He tried not to look at her chest as he pinned it on, but he was failing. *Ew.* That was one disadvantage to her newfound attractiveness. Every guy seemed like some version of J-Fro.

"I'll take that, thanks," Rachel snapped at him, and finished putting it on herself. She was perfectly capable of doing things on her own.

The main anchor, Rod Remington, was nearby. Rachel recognized him from watching the news each night; he had that classic smarmy newscaster look about him. A makeup woman was applying powder to his face. He smiled as he asked about her upcoming vacation to Boca Raton. She was blushing, clearly not immune to his sleazy charms. Rachel was pretty sure there was a clone of him at every news station in the country. Just a little *too* put together and witty. Parted hair that was going fashionably gray. A caricature of himself.

It had gone around the rumor mill at McKinley that Sue Sylvester herself had once been in a relationship with Rod. He'd ultimately cast her aside for his coanchor, Andrea Carmichael. Coach Sylvester didn't take it well. Yet she somehow managed to still work next to the two of them every week. Rachel guessed that being jilted by men was actually one topic she and Coach Sylvester could relate on. Too bad they weren't going to be discussing men today.

"On in five, everybody!" a fat guy in a headset shouted to the room. Everyone scrambled to their respective stations. Nearby, Kurt frantically motioned for Rachel to take her seat next to Coach Sylvester at the anchor desk. As she obliged, Rachel could tell that this was not going to be fun. She just had to get through it, though. To storm out now would just feed into her diva Scary Berry image.

It wasn't long until the theme music for *WOHN News 8* came blasting through the studio speakers. Coach Sylvester flashed the double finger guns at Rachel.

"You ready to wow western Ohio, Yoda?"

Rachel was getting really tired of the jabs implying she was so small. But that was Coach Sylvester. At least it was better than getting her hair constantly made fun of, like Mr. Schuester was. There was nothing Coach Sylvester hated more than Mr. Schuester's hair.

"Bring it," Rachel said through clenched teeth, and smiled sweetly back. Those coffees were really starting to kick in. This was kind of exciting! This was probably what it felt like to be on *Saturday Night Live.*

"Live in five! Four!" The man up front only motioned the last three numbers with his hand, then did a grand swooping gesture.

The ON AIR sign lit up neon-green.

"Good moooorning, Lima! I'm Rod Remington...." He looked over at his wife.

"And I'm Andrea Carmichael. Welcome to your nine o'clock news!" These anchors were a little too peppy for their own good. Especially at nine in the morning.

"Before we get to this morning's news, we have a very special edition of 'Sue's Corner,' " Rod continued. "A special guest has flown in all the way from the Big Apple to be with us today! Over to you, Sue." His words all ran together like an auctioneer. Why was he talking so fast? Maybe he had also just downed a few coffees.

The light on the camera in front of them lit up, signaling that they were now on-screen. Rachel straightened in her chair. She had to find a good place to dive in and say her piece.

"Thanks, A-Rod." Coach Sylvester took a long breath and began. "You know, there are a lot of books and movies out there that try to persuade the youth of our society to take care of one another, to nurture each other's talents and dreams. That it's all about teamwork—kissing each other's butts and changing each other's diapers. Western Ohio, I think it's time we ended this tradition of fairness and weakness and bring back what that good ole Mr. Darwin had to teach us. Survival. Of. The. Fittest. How are we ever supposed to weed out the nose-pickers, underachievers, and video game–playing pizza-faces if these kids are all looking out for *each other* instead of number one? You think you can win an international cheerleading competition through good sportsmanship? No. You win it by giving Team Belgium some yummy laxative-laced brownies. Works every time.

"As you can see, there is something to my left. No, no people—it's not a LEGO figurine. It's a person named Rachel Berry. She was one of my former students—you can't tell by her freakishly tiny frame, but this girl is a ruthless, dream-crushing machine. She doesn't care about petty things like 'others' feelings.' She has no hesitation about stomping on those around her to reach her lofty goals. I certainly never have, and look at me! That's right, viewers. You are looking at *two* of a kind. So, kids, take a tip from Rachel and me here and feel free to beat up anyone who gets in your way. May only the strong survive. And that's how Sue 'Cs' it!" She made a *C* shape with her hand as she said the last part.

Suddenly, Rachel began to panic. She had been so appalled by what Coach Sylvester was saying about her that she'd completely frozen! Maybe she could still get a word in really fast. "I'd just like to say that —"

Coach Sylvester interrupted her immediately. "Oh, forgot to mention the big end-of-year rally at McKinley High tomorrow. Show up to see a real winner in *person*," Coach Sylvester said with a smile. "And Rachel Berry will be there, too," she added quickly. Classic.

Then the camera light turned off. The segment was over. Rachel had totally blown it. Coach Sylvester's rant on caring for others had turned her into the poster child for selfishness. This was not going to help her case with any of the ex–Glee members at all. They already thought she was the worst. After watching "Sue's Corner," they probably wouldn't even talk to her again.

Rachel felt like such an idiot for thinking she could exonerate herself during "Sue's Corner." Coach Sylvester talked even faster than Rod Remington when she got going on one of her rants. There was no way Rachel was going to get to say anything at all. She stood up angrily and ripped the microphone off her shirt.

On the other side of the room, Rod and Andrea continued on with the news of the day. It mainly consisted of weather and traffic reports, but the main feature was yet another exposé on cow-tipping. It was really sad that there was nothing else going on in Lima besides farmyard shenanigans. Even worse was that Rachel just made a complete fool of herself in a place like that. It would all blow over soon, she hoped.

Rachel charged off the set, heading straight back to the dressing room to get her stuff. Coach Sylvester followed closely behind her. "Hey, not so fast, Polly Pocket. I wanted to say thank you." Was Coach Sylvester actually trying to be nice? Rachel wasn't falling for it. Coach Sylvester had just proven that everything she did had some underlying agenda attached to it.

Rachel picked up her leather bag and slung it over her shoulder. "It was nothing. I do much bigger talk shows than this all the time. You know, *national* ones." Or so Rachel had been told by Kurt. It didn't really matter if she didn't remember them at the present moment. She just wanted to show Coach Sylvester who had more fame and influence.

"No, you dim-witted hobbit. I wanted to thank you for getting that haircut known as Will Schuester gone from McKinley. I feel like I can finally walk down the halls again without running the risk of having my whole day ruined by the sight of an uncoordinated Michael Bublé impersonator who randomly breaks out into mid-nineties rap songs." She slapped Rachel on the back so hard that it forced her to stumble forward a few steps. "I guess it took the power of two talented ladies. You and me, kid. I should have enlisted you sooner."

Kurt entered the dressing room with caution. He looked like he was walking into the middle of a knife fight.

"I would have, but I thought you were one of those awful Glee kids through and through. Schuester's girl. Hah! If only he could see you now." Coach Sylvester smiled with delight at the thought of this.

"Why can't he?" Kurt asked, growing worried. "What happened to him? Ever since he left New York . . ." It sounded like Kurt knew more than he had been letting on.

"Does it matter, Porcelain?" Coach Sylvester put her hands on her hips. "The only thing that matters is that he's taken his weeds elsewhere to get whacked. I think my vision's gotten better since I don't have to look at those atrocious curls every day. Only have to wear one contact lens now." Coach Sylvester grabbed Kurt's hand, held it up, and forced him to high-five her. Then she left.

Rachel frantically searched her mind for anything she might have done to make Mr. Schuester leave, but nothing resurfaced. She was about to ask Kurt more about Mr. Schuester's allegedly having come to New York, but he immediately changed topics.

"That 'interview' was awful," he said. "We really need something to make up for this, otherwise everyone is really going to hate you — even more than they already do."

Kurt was right. But what could she possibly do to convince people that she wasn't cut from the same horrible cloth as Sue Sylvester?

"I've got it!" Kurt frantically opened his overstuffed organizer and began to flip through it. He located a magazine clipping from *Superstar Weekly* and passed it to Rachel with a hopeful look on his perfectly moisturized face. "This is what we have to do."

Rachel was missing something. She searched the picture for clues. It was of her alongside her two *Oklahoma!* costars, Meredith Stewart and Carmine Bennett. They were all dressed up. The caption below said that the photo was taken at their opening-night bash.

"What? We should throw a big party?" It *was* what the kids on the football team did when they wanted to be popular. It actually wasn't too bad of an idea. Of course, there was always the chance that none of her friends would come. It would be like her sixth birthday party all over again.

"No, of course not. There's no time to plan a really good party anyway." Kurt waved her idea away with his hand. He was getting impatient. He thought Rachel could be really dense sometimes, even if his suggestion had been really cryptic. "What do you do when you have a task that is too big to do on your own?"

"Still do it on my own?" Rachel said, in all seriousness. She didn't like asking for help.

"No, you call for reinforcements." He tapped the picture of Rachel, Meredith, and Carmine. "Let's have them come and perform with you at the rally! It's perfect! Everyone loves them. If they saw all three of you together, it would definitely grab their attention and win their hearts." Maybe that was pushing it. "Or just not be totally mad at you anymore."

It was an interesting theory. Rachel wasn't really sure that Kurt's plan would work, but she didn't have any other ideas. She was in no position to reject it. At this point, she just wanted her friends back.

"Do it," Rachel said. "Fly them in."

Kurt nodded his acknowledgment and immediately began making calls on his cell.

Maybe it wasn't too late to make amends. If not, at least Rachel would be surrounded by her new friends. Turns out, doing things alone wasn't all it was cracked up to be.

twelve

Chateau Lima, Wednesday night

It had been a long day. After the complete disaster of a television appearance on "Sue's Corner," Rachel and Kurt decided to take the afternoon off. They went to grab a nostalgic lunch at Breadstix. Even though there was a signed head shot of her on the wall (immediate points), Rachel regretted the decision upon discovering that Breadstix was still just as gross as it had always been. Kurt's spaghetti looked worse than her dad Leroy's (and he was a terrible cook). It was pretty hard to mess up spaghetti. The wilted leaves of the lettuce in her salad seemed like they had come from the same batch as the last salad she remembered eating there. Still gross.

Come to think of it, her last visit to the restaurant had been that night with Finn. They'd had a big fight over something silly—Rachel's refusal to participate in Mr. Schuester's music camp. Even though everyone kept talking about it like it was some big turning point, Rachel was still not sure she was convinced. Like teaching some snotty kids to sing had really changed their lives. It was completely absurd.

After lunch, they decided to just head back to the hotel. Kurt said he had a lot of work to do with coordinating travel arrangements for Meredith and Carmine. He also said something about an appointment, but he didn't let on about what it was for. He was being a little sketchy. Rachel shrugged it off—mainly because she had a lot of things to get done, too.

They had been so busy this week that she hadn't practiced her song for Thursday's show at all. It was very unlike her. She also wanted to look through the yearbook again. So far, it hadn't really told her much more than what people around school had told her.

The only interesting thing was that Sam Evans appeared to have become leader of the geeks or something. He started a World of Warcraft club and had taken over the Comic Book Enthusiasts Club as well. Rachel knew he had been into weird stuff, like speaking Navi, the alien language from the movie *Avatar*, last year. Maybe that's why he and Quinn broke up. They had made such a vanilla couple, anyway. What a difference a year makes.

It felt good to finally take control of the situation. Well, to have Kurt take control of the situation for Rachel. His idea to bring her famous costars in from New York was inspired. This way, the students at McKinley would not only associate her with being super-famous, but they would also see that she had great friends, too. Once they got to meet stars like Meredith Stewart and Carmine Bennett, they would stop seeing her as the Rachel Berry who'd abandoned them and begin to see her as the person putting Lima, Ohio, on the map. Which she totally was.

The only other famous person to ever come out of Lima was Phyllis Diller, the actress and comedienne. Rachel doubted that any of her friends even knew who she was, though. In truth, she only actually did because she had researched Phyllis obsessively to figure out how she'd escaped. Similar to Rachel, Phyllis had left her regular high school midway through in order to attend a fancy music conservatory in Chicago. Smart girl, Rachel had always thought. Now she wondered if Phyllis ever regretted leaving her friends behind. Were they jealous of her when she came back to visit them? Rachel made a mental note to get Phyllis Diller's contact information and see if she had any good advice for another brilliant actress from her humble hometown.

Rachel looked for the plastic key card to her suite. She really must stop carrying such large bags. It was impossible to find anything in them, even if they were trendy.

"Looking for something?" Rachel was startled to see Puck leaning casually against her hotel room door. In his hand was the room key.

"Give that to me, Puckerman!" Rachel snatched it from his hands. "How did you get that? Have you been stealing purses again?" She was not amused.

"No, of course not, babe. That's *my* copy. The chick at the front desk was no match for the Puckster's charms." He ran his fingers lightly over Rachel's bare arms. "She's a major fan of Mohawks. And general sexiness." Puck smoothed his hair down.

Rachel turned around and shot him a death stare. This guy was unbelievable. She ought to call the police on him for breaking and entering, though, technically, he hadn't broken anything yet. Or entered.

Rachel let her eyes wander over his tan biceps. "Why do you think you can just go around doing whatever you want all the time?"

"Why not? You do. And no one says anything."

She hadn't the slightest idea why he was here in the first place. It couldn't be for any respectable reason. Now he was insulting her? Rachel's sassy mode kicked in.

"Look, I don't know what you want. But I think you need to leave before I call to have you escorted off the premises."

"Dude, that's so not cool. I had to hitchhike all the way here from school. Have you ever ridden anywhere with Artie's mom?" He shook his head. "Unless you want to hear 'Dancing Queen' by ABBA on repeat, don't."

Rachel slid the card into the slot on the handle. The light flashed green, and she pushed down to open the door.

"Given our history, you can't blame me for being even the tiniest bit suspicious of your motives, Noah." She was starting to remember exactly how she had ended up in compromising situations with him before. Those brown eyes of his

146

really sucked a girl in. She tried not to make eye contact with him. It was hard.

"Aw, come on, Rachel. I just wanted to hang out. I really missed you all year. You were one of my best friends."

Rachel considered his sad puppy-dog expression before caving. He looked sincere enough. And he had said they were friends. She was running low on those right now.

"Oh, all right. I do need someone to listen to me practice."

They entered the suite, and Puck took in his new surroundings.

"Dude, seriously sweet pad." He took a running leap and dove onto Rachel's bed. The comforter rumpled, and several pillows fell onto the floor. "Nice bed, too. Huge." He bounced up and down.

"You are so predictable." Rachel pointed to the door. "Get out!"

"What? Big celebrities can't take jokes?"

Puck stood up and began shoddily rearranging the areas of the covers he'd messed up. He sucked at it. Puck had clearly never made a bed in his entire life, Rachel thought. Didn't they do those bed checks in juvie where they bounced a quarter off the bed to see if the sheets were tucked in tight enough? Or was that just military school?

"Don't get your pretty panties in a twist over it, dude." Puck always called everyone "dude," even when referring to their panties. It was weird.

She walked over and pulled the other side of the fluffy white comforter down taut.

"The only thing that's twisted is you, Puckerman." There was something extremely plush about all-white bedding. Total luxury. Too bad Puck had just gotten a dirty mark from his shoe on the bottom of the comforter. Now she was going to have to call down to the main desk to have them switch it out before bedtime. It was crazy how Puck managed to create trouble with even the smallest of actions.

"Sorry," he said sheepishly. "So it's totally crazy how you became all famous and stuff. I mean, I gotta admit — all those times you were saying stuff like that in Glee Club, I thought you were full of crap."

This didn't really surprise Rachel. No one had ever really understood her.

"What's it like, living like a baller?" Puck asked as he wandered into the jewelry box of a living room.

His amazement at their surroundings made Rachel realize just how quickly she'd acclimated to her new life of luxury. It was bizarre that Rachel had grown so used to the fancy furnishings that she hardly even noticed them anymore. Maybe this stuff didn't matter as much as she'd thought it would. Or maybe it was impossible for her to be happy with whatever she had at the present moment. Even if it *was* pretty.

Puck wandered around, probably calculating the cost of each item and what he could get for it on craigslist. His bad-boy looks created an interesting juxtaposition in the classy room, like a smoldering rock star who was about to trash the place. It was actually hot. Rachel tried to act casual but began to experience a weird nervousness bubbling up inside of her.

"It's enjoyable, I suppose...." she said, restlessly pacing among the various pieces of furniture.

Puck lay down on the chaise lounge like a therapy patient who was about to spill his heart out.

In an attempt to occupy her hands, Rachel picked up a shiny gold pillow from the couch and began to nervously fiddle with one of the corner tassels.

"But to be honest, lately I've been having trouble recalling much about my life in New York. I don't know what it is. Maybe I'm just nervous being back here." She looked down at him. Puck's shirt was coming up a little, revealing his perfect abs. Rachel quickly diverted her eyes. "You know, old feelings getting drummed up and all that." It was probably better to change the subject. "Do you ever talk to Mr. Schuester?"

"Naw. Haven't seen the dude since the beginning of the year. I heard he left to, like, go hook up with you. Is that true?" Puck bolted upright. "Are you and Mr. Schu dating?" His eyes widened in disbelief.

Rachel had never heard anything so ridiculous. Sure, she had once harbored a crush on Mr. Schuester. He was a cute teacher. Plus, he had a little bit of an older Justin Timberlake thing going on with his crooning and smooth moves. But it was just an innocent schoolgirl crush. She would never actually consider dating him. He was so old!

"Of course not!" Rachel threw the gold pillow at Puck's face. It hit him right in the nose. Rachel couldn't help but laugh.

"Oh, you did *not* just do that." A devious smile began to form on Puck's face. "You are going down, Berry!" He grabbed a teal sequined pillow and started to chase her around the room with it held high above his head. She squealed in mock protest. He caught up with her and threw the pillow at her face. It felt as if it were the first time Rachel had laughed in days.

The next thing she knew, there were throw pillows everywhere, and the two of them were full-on making out on the couch. Things had escalated so fast! But this wasn't the first time she'd ever kissed Puck. Rachel decided to not overthink it for once and just have fun. Besides, he was extremely skilled.

He rubbed her back seductively, and Rachel shivered. *Wow.*

So he'd had an agenda. Big deal. It wasn't exactly hidden. And some part of Rachel must have wanted this to happen if she'd allowed him to come into the suite. A girl didn't just invite Puck into her room if she didn't want to get hit on. It was practically a given.

Click! Click! That was a weird noise. It was probably just a text message from Kurt. Rachel continued to kiss Puck, letting her mind go blissfully blank.

Click! Rachel opened an eye long enough to see Puck holding up a digital camera, snapping off a series of photos. *Click!* She couldn't believe it. He was documenting their make-out session!

"What do you think you are doing?" Rachel screamed as

she shoved his burly frame off of her. Rachel snatched the camera out of his hand. "I can't believe you were taking pictures of me...and you...while we were..." Rachel readjusted her shirt, which was now almost completely twisted around backward.

"Well, let's see what we've got here, shall we?" She pushed the VIEW button on Puck's camera. The first frame was blurry—clearly, he wasn't too good at feeling someone up and taking pictures of her at the same time. The next few shots were of Rachel's chest.

"Rachel," he pleaded, "I'm sorry! I was totally just trying to get a good shot of your Joobs."

She knew this shirt was doing wonders, but she didn't want some gross photos of her in it. If she were ever going to have pictures like this taken, it would be when she was way older. And in a classy publication, like *GQ* or a similar magazine. They wouldn't look skanky, like these.

Puck's words finally registered with her.

"My what?" Puck was always making up words.

"You know, *Joobs*," he said, as if emphasizing the same word would make her understand it. "Jew boobs. I was also trying to get shots of other parts of you, too. If that makes you feel better."

He smiled at her and tried to pull her back to him. She took two more steps away from where he was sitting.

"As flattered as I am, *no*. That does *not* make me feel better." Rachel continued to click through the pictures, which were all of her. They were taken from various angles and all from different occasions that week. Places she hadn't even seen Puck. He had been *stalking* her. How creepy. "What are these all for? Your own amusement?" She shuddered as she said it. That was so not something she wanted to think about.

Puck stood up. "I only did it because I had to, man! A guy's gotta make a living somehow!"

A living? Had Puck become an amateur paparazzo?

"Are you selling these?"

Puck strolled over to the minibar and looked inside the fridge. He grabbed a beer and popped it open with the crook of his arm. "Maybe. J-Fro and I have a little Rachel Berry website.... It's kind of a big deal. I'm surprised you haven't heard of it, actually. It's the best one on the Web, and the fans have been begging for some Joob shots." His eyes focused on her chest region. "I came in to do the job because no one else could deliver. I was even offering one hundred bucks for the best shot! Can't believe everyone failed." Puck sipped his beer.

What a jerk. Rachel clicked through the camera menu until she saw the DELETE ALL button. She punched it without hesitation.

"Get out." She stormed to the door and opened it, casually tossing Puck's camera out into the hallway. She heard a crash.

"No!" Puck yelled as he chased after it. "That thing was, like, two hundred bucks!"

Rachel slammed the door behind him. She took a few

deep breaths to help her rage subside. The events of the last hour had cost her not only her dignity, but also a beer from the minibar. That one beer probably cost about ten dollars, if what she'd always heard about minibars was true. Puck was truly evil. Preying on her vulnerability like that. She cursed herself for falling for it again.

Rachel got ready for bed in a horrible mood. She removed her makeup with a cotton ball and thought about all the people in Lima who were only out to get her. She must have had some reason for wanting to come back here, but at the present moment nothing came to mind. Rachel grabbed the floss dispenser and unwound a large piece. Being upset about something was no reason to ignore one's gums.

Everything that had happened during the trip so far was weighing heavily on her mind, and she still had no information on Mr. Schuester's whereabouts. Rachel wasn't sure why, but she was actually starting to worry about him. Sue Sylvester had said he had left. Kelly Mahoney had said he'd gone to New York. So had Puck. But then again, Puck had also thought Rachel was dating Mr. Schuester. Puck wasn't a very reliable source of information—unless the thing you were trying to find out had to do with the best way to steal bags of tortilla chips from the mini-mart. Oh well, it was out of her hands for now, and Rachel didn't really have time to worry about her sad, old Glee Club supervisor when there were more urgent matters to attend to that directly affected her own dignity.

Once her dental hygiene and moisturizing routines were

complete, Rachel climbed into her giant bed and flipped open her laptop. She had to see this alleged Rachel Berry website. It didn't take her long to find it — it was called "J-Fro and Puck's Site of Juicy Rachel Berry Hotness." A little bit of her previous anger dissipated when she saw that. Rachel liked to have her ego stroked. Even though there were some creepy shots of her sleeping or without makeup, she looked amazing in most of them. And there were a lot of them.

Twenty minutes had soon passed. Browsing the site was just so much fun! The layout was surprisingly professional (more likely J-Fro's expertise than Puck's), and the pictures made her look incredible. Also, it was done up entirely in her favorite bold colors — red, yellow, and blue. There were gold stars everywhere. That creeper J-Fro sure knew her well. In the corner, there was a little banner that said NEW SITE COMING SOON!

She was starting to feel as if maybe the website wasn't such a bad thing. Part of being famous meant having fan sites dedicated to her. And this one was great, even if Puck was paying people to take scandalous pictures of her without her permission.

Her stomach turned. There was a photo that stopped her in her tracks. It was of Rachel, staring out the window of her jetBerry plane. There was only one person who could have taken that picture. He was the one person who was supposed to be her closest confidante and most trusted employee.

And his name was Kurt Hummel. Mercedes had called it right a few days ago. What a *gator*.

thirteen

Principal Figgins's office, Thursday morning

Principal Figgins was having quite the week. The end of the school year was always a busy time for teachers and administrators, but this year's final week had been especially stressful. It was mostly because of all the extra performers scheduled for the end-of-year rally. They were drawing a ton of local media attention, and Figgins was getting at least ten calls a day about them. He was pretty sure that half of those calls were from his mother, but his secretary, Mrs. Goodrich, wouldn't admit to it. She would just lean in and say "We got another one, sir" before going back to her knitting. Right now she was working on a purple sweater for one of her cats.

He was relieved that the last day of school was tomorrow. After the rally was over and the decorations were packed away for the summer, all he had to worry about was the graduation ceremony the following week, which was already being overshadowed by Rachel Berry's celebrated return to McKinley High.

The students had been buzzing with excitement about having Miss Berry roam the halls all week long. She looked so sophisticated and metropolitan in her fancy clothes and such. Normally, Figgins didn't like to make examples of students who had dropped out of school, but he was willing to make an exception for Rachel. She had become very famous, which had meant lots of good press for the school and its arts programs. The rally this afternoon was sure to be another example to the community of what a great school Figgins was running here. Maybe he would even be nominated for district principal of the year. He'd always hoped to attend the swanky dinner banquet at the Chateau Lima. It was going to happen one of these years. He just knew it.

Although most of McKinley's extracurricular programs were thriving, Glee Club had taken quite the nosedive in popularity and overall quality since Rachel's departure. But it didn't matter—Figgins could always find holes to fill in the school budget. If students were no longer interested in singing and dancing, he could put in a new soda machine by the gym. It was also a relief not to have to deal with the constant bickering from Sue Sylvester and Will Schuester, now that the Glee Club maestro had taken off. They had always been arguing over petty things, like where the excess Cheerios trophies should be kept. Sue had insisted that they go in the choir room, but Will had thought it was disrespectful. Figgins couldn't have cared less either way. Those two used to give him a constant headache.

Figgins popped his head outside the glass door that separated his desk from Mrs. Goodrich's.

"Did you say I had an appointment with someone at nine or ten?" It was already five minutes past nine, and Mrs. Goodrich often mixed up times. She wasn't that great of a secretary. But she had several cat mouths to feed, so he kept her on. Figgins could be a softie.

She looked up from her knitting. "Rachel Berry at nine. Santana Lopez at ten." Ah, that was right. He'd forgotten that the two were scheduled back to back. Normally, he wouldn't worry about two appointments that were an hour apart possibly running into each other, but Rachel Berry always had a lot to say. And she was already late.

"Sorry I'm late!" Rachel chirped as she burst into the office. Kurt Hummel was in tow. She was wearing a revealing red-and-navy-blue-striped minidress. Kurt matched her in a white suit. They looked like they were going to a Fourth of July garden party in the Hamptons rather than parading through the corridors of McKinley High. Overdressed for the occasion, as per usual.

"Good morning, children." Figgins knew that teenagers weren't children, but for some reason he was never able to call them anything else. It had earned him many spiteful looks from students throughout the years. "Please come inside."

Rachel was feeling much better after a good night's rest.

The events of the previous day had shaken her up, but this morning she'd woken up feeling confident about the performance. Especially with the addition of her New York friends, which was why she was here. She thought it was only fair to come early this morning to let the principal know about her guests. It wouldn't be polite to spring that on him three minutes before they went onstage. This also gave him a few hours to hire extra security guards or maybe call a field reporter from *Extra*.

"Thanks for seeing us at the last minute, Principal Figgins," Rachel began. She was careful not to let anything slip as she took a seat opposite him. There was an art to sitting in short dresses. Many young stars in Hollywood had not perfected it yet. Practically every week, a different starlet was photographed flashing something she hadn't meant to — Rachel was not going to be one of those girls. "We just wanted to let you know that some extra guests will be joining us for my performance this afternoon. You *do* know Meredith Stewart and Carmine Bennett, right?"

Figgins hesitated to answer the question. He was a huge Meredith Stewart fan. Maybe the biggest there was. Reruns of her first show on the CW, *Double Exposure* — about a fashion model who moonlights as a butt-kicking double agent for the CIA — was one of his greatest guilty pleasures. And Carmine Bennett used to be in a popular music group. He was now the face of the cologne Mrs. Figgins had given him for his birthday, Virile: For Men. She said it made him smell like George Clooney.

"Sure, I think I have heard of them," Figgins answered nonchalantly. Excitement bubbled up inside him. This rally was shaping up to be the best McKinley had ever seen. So many stars in one place! "Your friends, of course, are welcome here. You will be excited to know that another special alumna has agreed to perform as well!"

Rachel's ears perked up. She didn't know anything about this at all! Who could the mysterious guest be? She racked her brain for any kids from previous years who might have gone off and become successful by some random twist of fate. She couldn't think of anyone. There was no way it could be someone more famous than she was. But maybe it was Phyllis Diller. That would be good because she had been dying to ask her some questions....

"Is that so?" Rachel said to Figgins, and gave Kurt's foot a sharp kick. He looked up from the text message he was sending. "What? Is something happening? I wasn't listening, because I was bored."

"I was just saying that *Santana Lopez* has agreed to perform in the rally as well!" Figgins looked at Kurt. "Isn't it great news?"

It had to be a joke. Rachel laughed, as it was only polite to laugh when someone tried to make jokes. Even if they were really bad ones. "You're kidding, right?" The color drained from Rachel's face. She was already pretty pale to begin with — now she looked like Robert Pattinson in *Twilight*.

"You wish he was," Santana's voice answered. There she stood, in the glass doorway, looking mighty fine. She was dressed in some futuristic metallic shorts and a red blouse with shoulder pads. It looked like an outfit that Nicki Minaj's stylist might have chosen, yet it worked on her.

"Hey, Figgins Newton. Where should I park my jet?" Santana laughed heartily as she watched Rachel's expression of simple shock transform into something much darker. "I'm kidding — only an idiot would spend their entire fortune on a private jet. Do you know what the gas mileage is like on those babies?" Santana put her hand on Rachel's shoulder. "Not good. But you already know that. Not to mention the carbon footprint." Santana glanced down at Rachel's footwear. "Hey, dwarf. You haven't grown at all, I see. Trying to wear big-girl shoes, though. Good for you!" Santana had learned the art of insulting someone for absolutely no reason from her former cheerleading coach. She turned to Kurt. "Nice job on her. She's slightly less painful to look at now."

Kurt avoided Rachel's eyes. "It's been a difficult road, but thank you. Excellent shorts." Kurt was looking at Santana as if she were Heidi Klum. He probably wished he were her stylist. "Your dress at the Grammys was epic." Santana had worn a gorgeous purple number by Monique Lhuillier. It had tons of ruffles. Kurt loved ruffles.

"What?" Rachel was sure she'd misheard Kurt's last statement. "Why would *you* be at the Grammys?"

The conversation had started to make Principal Figgins, who was still sitting at his desk, really uncomfortable. His least favorite part of being a high school principal was when teenage girls started to pick fights with each other. They always did that creepy move that made them look like bobblehead dolls. It was supposed to convey attitude, Mercedes Jones had told him once. He generally began walking the other way if he saw someone doing that.

"Why don't I leave you two big stars in here to catch up? I'm just going to go to the teachers' lounge for some fresh coffee," Figgins interjected before making a quick exit.

Santana crossed over to the other side of the room to face Rachel and Kurt. She propped one arm on the desk in front of her and leaned forward to answer Rachel's question.

"Because you're not the only celeb up in this place, Thumbelina." Santana knew her angles well. The pose accentuated the boob job she'd gotten two summers ago. It had been silly. Santana didn't need surgical enhancements at all—she was already gorgeous.

It was sad just how far some girls would go to get noticed. But Rachel didn't need to cut herself up to be successful. When one had talents, they spoke for themselves. Just look at Barbra Streisand. Casting directors told her that she would have to get a nose job to become more bankable as an actress. She refused because it would mess up her singing voice. Now she was one of the most successful actresses of all time.

"Oh, did you sign up for one of those seat-filler tickets? You know, the kind where the real celebrity gets up to pee and you sit down in their seat while they are gone?" Rachel asked. Awards shows often used this tactic to create an illusion of a full theater.

One year, Rachel had begged her dads to let her sign up

161

for the seat-filler job. They said no because Los Angeles was way too far to travel to. She pouted for days afterward. But none of that mattered now. Rachel would have her own seat-filler at the Grammys soon.

"Like you don't know that I'm actually, like, über-famous now. Does the Best New Artist category ring a bell?" Santana made air quotes with her fingers as she said it. Her nails were painted a fiery red. "It's been quite the whirlwind. You know — parties...hot guys...VIP status everywhere I go. I get so much free stuff, too — it's baller." She looked at Kurt. "I have some skinny jeans from Seven For All Mankind that would totes fit you if you want them."

Kurt salivated. "Oh yes, please."

"I don't understand how this happened!" Rachel said, as if wishing something weren't true would make it so. She did this a lot. "You do have a decent voice, to be sure, but it's certainly not star quality. And you've never had any goals other than getting more notches on your bedpost than Brittany."

Santana smirked devilishly. "Oh, honey, I reached that one long ago. Parties at Lady Gaga's mansion can really up a girl's number, if you know what I mean."

Rachel resisted the urge to slap her.

Santana continued. "You know, Rachel, you really should be nicer to people. You never know whose dad is going to turn out to be a major record producer."

It was funny that Santana of all people was giving a lecture on the merits of kindness to strangers. Rachel was pretty sure she'd seen Santana steal from a canned-food drive once. That girl had no place to talk.

"For once, one of Schuester's dumb ideas worked out." She paused and reconsidered her word choice. "Well, it worked out for *me*."

Rachel couldn't bear the way she was dancing around the subject. Santana knew that drawing out the information was killing Rachel, so naturally she wanted it to last as long as possible.

"What on earth are you talking about? Just spill it, Santana."

Out in the hall, first period had just ended. Students swarmed the halls, and a little crowd of spectators began to gather outside Figgins's office. The transparent glass walls had given them away. Everyone wanted to catch a glimpse of the new star. Santana flashed a megawatt smile at the group and waved. Not to be outdone, Rachel stood up and did the same.

Santana picked up one of Figgins's brass owls and mind-lessly began to rub it. She was a very tactile person. "So last summer at that, like, awful hippie music camp thing — there was this little girl named Megan, right? She was obsessed with me." She struck a few more poses for the kids outside. A dweeby kid in a brown baseball cap was transfixed. He looked like a zombie waiting to pounce on her the second she left her glass safe haven.

"She followed me around everywhere and stuff. At first I

was all, 'Ew. A kid.' But then I was all, 'I can make her do my bidding.' " Santana tousled her dark hair and blew a kiss at the crowd outside. "I've always wanted a tiny person pet."

"Um, I'm pretty sure that's child abuse." Rachel hoped this story had a point. Listening to Santana was exhausting. But Kurt was rapt with attention.

"Is it? Whatever. Anyway, this kid Megan was always begging me to sing with her. She wanted the two of us to do a song about angels for her dad. I think it was about her dead mom or something. So I felt bad and did it and . . ."

"And then he turned out to be Peter Smithson, the famous record producer," Kurt finished. "People are calling him the next David Foster."

Rachel knew who he was. She'd read that Smithson had been responsible for fourteen number-one singles in the past year alone. Talk about luck.

"Even though my debut album, *Saint Santana*, just dropped and I'm planning a national tour, I had to make a little time to come back and steal your thunder. I just couldn't resist!" Santana patted Rachel on the head. "Isn't it cute that the fans call me Saint Santana? Peter thinks it's because of all the charity work I do. I don't know why I didn't figure it out sooner, but karma, like, totally works."

Rachel was horrified. Santana was the last person on Earth who should be exalted for her attitude toward others. That was like praising Sue Sylvester for her fashion sense. It was absurd and unacceptable.

"This was fun, guys! Now if you'll excuse me, I have to go

brag about my newfound fame and fortune to anyone who will listen." Santana strutted to the door.

Before leaving, she mouthed "call me" to Kurt as she held an invisible phone to her ear. She then yelled out, "Later, bitches!" much to the shock of Mrs. Goodrich, who'd fallen asleep at her desk. Mornings weren't really her thing.

Rachel felt sick as she watched the students swarming Santana, asking for autographs and pictures. They looked way more excited than when they'd seen Rachel. This was a disaster.

"You knew about this?" Rachel shot at Kurt. He'd seemed a little too calm about the whole situation.

"Well, I do read the blogs, yes," Kurt answered. "There were some rumors of a surprise Santana Lopez appearance. But honestly, I thought she'd be way too busy to bother! She must really want to show you up."

Like that was any consolation. Whose side was he on anyway?

The happy, determined feeling Rachel had woken up with was quickly dissolving into misery. How had Santana managed to achieve everything that Rachel had worked her entire life for so fast? Karma was definitely not the greater force at work here. If it were, Santana would be getting ready to start a lifelong job at the Lima Freeze, not attending awards shows and glitzy music-industry parties. The cherry on top of this icy news was that the media were portraying Santana as a saint! Peter Smithson had probably coined the term himself as part of his grand plan to make her a star.

Kurt could see how upset Rachel was. "Don't worry, Rach. People totally just think she's Jennifer Lopez's little sister. That's why her album is doing so well on the charts." It was nice of him to try to console Rachel. "If it makes you feel any better, she's totally going to have to get butt implants if she wants to keep up the Lopez theory."

It was all so ridiculous that Rachel had to laugh. The two of them were no longer students at McKinley High, yet here they were again, competing for the spotlight. Nothing ever changed.

"Forget about Santana," Kurt said, standing up and reaching out to her. "Now, let's go get your famous besties and put on a real Broadway-quality show."

"Yes, let's." Rachel still hadn't confronted Kurt about selling her out to Puck. She was waiting for the right time. Trouble was, there was never really a great opportunity to accuse someone of stabbing you in the back, especially when you needed them. She'd deal with that later. For now, she had to focus on winning. Because whether or not anyone else knew it, the rally had just become a competition. And Scary Berry didn't lose. Especially not to anyone named Saint Santana. It was on.

fourteen

McKinley High gymnasium, before the rally,
Thursday afternoon

All afternoon, throngs of people had been arriving at the school to stake out seats for the big show. Because none of the previous years' rallies had ever been a community event, there was no precedent for what to do with all the extra bodies. The majority of the attendees were people who had caught yesterday's edition of "Sue's Corner." Many were hoping to witness some sort of live Rachel Berry breakdown.

By noon, the gym was already packed to its full capacity, and the students hadn't even been let out of their classes yet. Prinicipal Figgins had to call in the help of the boys' varsity basketball team to scour the school for extra folding chairs. It didn't help much. Usually whenever they were given a group task, three of them tried while the rest kept busy giving each other atomic wedgies.

If the local fire marshal were to drop in to the gym for a random inspection, he would definitely not approve. But with any luck, the only disaster that would befall the crowd at McKinley was the upcoming interpretative song-and-dance performance by Brittany Pierce's bizarre Glee Club, New New Directions. They were an odd bunch. Not that anyone was thinking about them at the present moment.

A tidal wave of excitement had taken over the gym. One of the moms from the Cheerios Booster Club had announced to her friends that her daughter had seen Santana Lopez by the foreign language wing. The news spread like brushfire through the bleachers. Soon, everyone was buzzing about the possibility of a Rachel Berry/Santana Lopez sing-off.

Back in the choir room, the acts were warming up. A makeshift dressing room had been created using a hodgepodge design of ropes and curtains. It looked more like a child's pillow fort than a greenroom fit for world-famous celebrities. But it was all the school had to offer.

The kids from New New Directions were busy getting into their weird-looking costumes. Rachel couldn't figure out what they were supposed to be. Eggplants? Barney the Friendly Dinosaur? The getups involved foam structures over glittery purple spandex bodysuits. If you squinted a little, they kind of resembled giant starfish.

"I wish I could pull off leggings," Brittany lamented, pinching the spandex with her fingers. Even though Brittany had chosen the outfits herself, she was having issues. "No, seriously. How do I get these off?"

When they first arrived, Brittany had proudly shown both Santana and Rachel to their own separate corners of the room. They each had a mirror propped up against the wall and a little stool. Rachel recognized them as the same ones used for school pictures every year. It was fancy digs.

"Sorry, Rachel. I'd stay, but I have to go get in a quick make-out session before we go onstage. It relaxes me," Brittany said as she closed Rachel's curtain, which was actually a William McKinley High fleece blanket clothespinned to a piece of twine. "Unless you want to come, too?" she said, peeping her blond head back in. Brittany didn't want to be rude.

"Um, no, thanks," Rachel said. "I have to warm up my vocal cords."

"Your loss, I'm ... awesome." Brittany shrugged and walked away. Rachel wouldn't be surprised if she was headed toward Santana's area to accomplish her goal. The two of them had always been ... close.

Rachel took in her reflection in the mirror. She looked absolutely amazing. She wore the sequined dress that she'd picked on the plane. Before Kurt had gone off to pick up Meredith and Carmine, he had helped her choose the perfect gold eye shadow to match. Combined with the wing-tip liquid liner she'd perfected, it made her eyes look big and bright. Her shiny, dark tresses were blown out to perfection, and her skin glowed. Absolutely gorgeous.

So why was she feeling so upset? She was about to go onstage (well, on court) and perform for hundreds of adoring fans. They'd shown up just to see her. It was everything she'd ever wanted. It didn't really matter that Santana had it, too. The two of them were about as similar as a parachute and a chicken taco.

Just as an athlete must stretch before a big game or race, it was important for a singer to ease into her routine. Rachel began humming. It was her favorite way to get started. She started to go into a series of elaborate noises. *Brrrrrr!* she trilled.

But as great as the little dressing room was, it wasn't soundproof. A group of Glee kids began to laugh at some unknown joke. Rachel could barely *think* in there with all the preshow activity, let alone get in a good warm-up. She had to get out of there. Fast.

She ran out into the hallway.

There was a janitor's closet nearby where she might be able to snag a few quiet moments to herself before it was time to go on. Rachel looked down at the ground as she ran. It was a vain attempt at remaining anonymous to the stragglers heading toward the gym, as well as at keeping her balance in her strappy gold stilettos. She pivoted on the ball of her foot to turn the corner. *Smack!*

All of a sudden, Rachel found herself cradled in Finn's strong arms.

"Rachel," he said, holding her up. Her name on his lips sounded like butter. And being in his arms again was starting to make her melt. My goodness, his biceps had gotten big.

"Finn! Oh, I'm so sorry. I was just, uh…um…" Her brain began to resemble the static on the old television set she and her dads used to keep in the basement.

Finn smiled warmly. "You weren't trying to leave again, were you? We just got you back." His eyes sparkled. "Are you okay?"

Rachel realized she had just been staring at him and not saying anything.

"Oh, uh, yes! I'm great! Why wouldn't I be?" She laughed nervously. Rachel couldn't remember why they'd ever broken up. She couldn't even remember *how* they'd broken up. Her heart sped up, and she started to break into a sweat. Good thing she'd just put on her extra-strength deodorant. She was also really glad that if she had to have an awkward meeting with an ex-boyfriend, this is what she was wearing while doing it. She couldn't have planned a better reunion outfit. Well, she actually had only sort of planned it. Or rather, Kurt had.

"Well, you look great. I'm so happy for you! I mean… Broadway — wow! If anyone could do it, Rachel, it's you."

Finn was being so nice. He was always so nice.

There was a pureness in him that so many boys lacked. Santana had once called it his "Finnocence." Rachel wouldn't dare give her the satisfaction of telling her so, but she'd thought it was clever at the time.

"Thanks. You seem like you're doing well, too," Rachel

171

said, steadying herself against a set of lockers. Ever since she had seen him with Quinn the other day, she hadn't been able to shake the image from her mind. Especially that forehead kiss.

Finn ran his fingers through his hair. It was one of his flirting moves. "Yeah. Pretty much!" He laughed, but there was a nervous quality to it.

Maybe he still liked her a little! Rachel's sweaty palms were proof that feelings didn't just completely go away.

"What have you been up to this year?" Rachel knew she should be warming up her voice instead of conversing with Finn, but she didn't want this to end.

"Well, I've been busy. You know, senior year and all that. And I've got Youth Group. After I worked with those awesome kids all summer at Mr. Schuester's camp, I felt so good. I wanted to do more good stuff. So Quinn signed me up at her church. It's awesome."

Finn had a limited vocabulary, but he meant well.

"Hey, you should come!"

Rachel laughed uncomfortably. "Ah, no, thanks....I'm Jewish, remember?" Finn had forgotten a major detail about her. Like she was some stranger. Ouch.

"Oh, right...of course you are." Finn looked embarrassed. "Well, if you wanted, you could still come and help teach some of the kids a song. I bet they would love it. A big star singing with them! They'd think it was awesome."

Rachel wanted to change the subject. She tore her eyes away from his face and let them drift to the large cross and the loopy QUINN tattoos on his forearm. Seeing the ink on his skin made her feel queasy. "Tattoos, huh? That's pretty permanent, Finn."

"Yeah, I know. Crazy, right?" Finn didn't seem like he thought it was all that crazy. She'd never seen him look so secure. "Quinn and I are really happy now. I think we just both needed a little time apart to grow up."

Rachel nodded in mock agreement.

"Well, you'd better get back to your warm-up," Finn said. "Good luck out there! Can't wait." He squeezed her arm reassuringly and took off toward the gym. He had only taken a few steps when he turned around and looked back at her. "Hey, Rachel?"

Rachel's heart skipped a beat. Was he about to tell her he was still madly in love with her? She took a deep breath. "Yes?"

Finn's words spilled out fast. "I just wanted to say I'm sorry for trying to pressure you into changing your plans last summer. You were right after all. Everything has turned out exactly how it should."

Rachel wasn't really so sure about that anymore, but she didn't protest.

"I know we didn't leave things on the best note, but I hope we can be friends," Finn continued. "Maybe I'll see you later...." Then he continued on his merry way down to the gym.

Friends, huh? I really screwed that one up, Rachel thought. She didn't even feel like warming up now.

Luckily, salvation came in the form of Kurt Hummel. He

walked in, leading Meredith Stewart and Carmine Bennett. They looked fantastic for having just gotten off a plane. Their outfits were variations of Rachel's own gold frock, employing both sequins and their own personal styles. Meredith wore a frilly gold skirt and white tank cinched together with a wide, black leather belt. Her black high heels elongated her supermodel legs. She was like a sexy giraffe. Carmine's skinny black tie, designer jeans, and gold wing-tipped shoes made him look like Michael Bublé. Mr. Schuester probably would have seriously coveted the look. Together, the three of them were going to make quite the trio. Kurt had style down to a science.

Rachel was starstruck for a brief moment as the three of them approached her. Then she remembered they were supposed to be her new best friends. Her costars on Broadway. How exciting! She felt like she was meeting them again for the first time.

Rachel couldn't form words. They all stood in a moment of awkward silence as Rachel mulled everything over.

Kurt tried to get her to say something. "Judy? Liza?" He poked her. "Patti LuPone?"

Rachel shook herself out of the trance. "Oh, sorry. Hi!"

Meredith spoke fast and furiously. "Okay, Rach, *puh-lease* tell me you did not call us all the way out here to the *boonies* to help you fulfill some desperate childish need to prove your success to a bunch of midwestern high school students and soccer moms because none of them ever believed in you before." Her tone was not friendly. But she had hit the nail right on the head.

"Of course not," Rachel shot back.

Carmine yawned. "Is this about an ex-boyfriend? Want me to beat him up? Want me to kiss you in front of him?" He stretched lazily. "When can we go home? I miss New York. This place smells like fried food and unrealized dreams."

For someone so good-looking, he was quite annoying to have around. It'd be better if he didn't talk.

After glancing at his surroundings, Carmine pulled out his cell phone and started texting someone. Approximately three seconds later, Meredith's phone buzzed. She read the text and cackled. Then they both looked at Rachel and burst into a fit of giggles again.

"Riiiight?" Carmine said, glancing from Meredith to Rachel.

"Oh my God, *so* right," Meredith agreed, trying to contain herself.

Rachel didn't understand the private joke, but she was pretty sure it was about her. Well, at least they were having fun. They both looked really out of place standing in the hallway at McKinley High, even though they couldn't be much older than she was. Very hip and urban. Not at all Ohio. This is what people probably saw when they looked at her and Kurt now.

Kurt butted in. "You guys really need to go finish getting ready."

Kurt was right — they were running out of time before the show was going to start. Rachel interrupted their text-fest.

"Yeah. Thanks for coming, you guys. It was really nice of you to make the trip. I really appreciate it a lot!" Rachel said sweetly. Meredith and Carmine looked at her like she had two heads.

"Who are you, and what have you gone and done with Rachel Scary?" Carmine said, playing with Rachel's hair. "You are trying to be nice, and it's really cute."

"Looks like little Dorothy is back in Kansas!" Meredith howled. "There's no place like home, right? You are definitely weird here, Rach. Let's go do this thing and get back to the city."

"Dressing room is that way," Kurt said, pointing them down the hall toward the choir room. "Don't get anything on your clothes! And if you see someone with a slushie, run!" Meredith and Carmine strutted off toward the dressing room, arm in arm. The two of them reminded Rachel of the way Brittany and Santana used to act with each other. "You should probably go with them. Make sure they don't terrorize any children or break anything."

Rachel turned to leave. Then she realized this was the perfect opportunity to confront Kurt.

"Wait —" Rachel said, looking him in the eyes. He looked so innocent. Maybe she was wrong. . . . No, her instincts hadn't failed her so far. "I have something I want to get off my chest before I go out there."

Kurt raised his eyebrows, intrigued. "Oh?"

"Yes." Rachel stuck her nose up in the air and looked away dramatically. She looked like she was about to deliver a Shakespearean monologue. "I know what you've been doing behind my back." A moment passed. It was always better to add in strategic pauses when interrogating a criminal. She'd learned that tidbit from watching *Law & Order* reruns when she was home sick with laryngitis. A well-placed moment of silence often had the power to bring about a confession.

"Ummm...buying you tons of amazing clothes and keeping your busy life organized?" Kurt offered with a shrug. He put his bag down and began looking for something inside it.

"No, the other thing." Rachel crossed her arms to show that she meant business. "Come on! You've been selling my personal photos to J-Fro and Puckerman for extra dough!" She threw her arms up in the air. "How could you? I saw that one from the plane on their website!"

Kurt's face showed no signs of remorse whatsoever. "Yeah, I totally did. Your point is?" He shrugged.

Rachel's lip quivered. "I thought you were supposed to be my friend! Those are...private." She was in a very fragile emotional state. It had been a tough week.

But now it was Kurt's turn to be mad. After everything they'd been through, Rachel still only thought about herself.

"Look, Rachel. Those pictures were going to get out any-way. Why shouldn't I be the one who benefits from them? You pay me practically nothing. You think it's easy for me to watch you get your dream role on Broadway? I keep hanging around, hoping you'll help me out with some sort of chance to audition or perform." His voice started to crack. "But you never do."

Kurt picked up his satchel from the floor. "So you think I'm a bad friend? Where do you think I learned this behavior?" he said, clenching his jaw angrily. "That's right. From *you*." He stormed down the hall and out the double doors leading to the entrance.

Rachel was completely stunned. First Kurt had stolen her pictures. Now he'd stolen her exit. But there was no one left for Rachel Berry to storm out on. She somehow kept finding herself alone.

fifteen

Choir room, minutes before the rally,
Thursday afternoon

The students at McKinley were not accustomed to so much excitement at once. Before this week, the most thrilling thing that had happened all year was when one of the science geeks, Stephanie Ruben, had mixed a brand-new flavor of slushie for the cafeteria. The magical lime-kiwi-raspberry creation had been so delicious that kids would get to school early just to buy one. The flavor sold out every morning before nine. It wasn't long before every student in the entire school was addicted to it. It became a problem. The kids were so wired on sugar that nothing ever got done in class. The Glee kids liked it because no one wanted to waste precious slushie on them, so their clothes remained dry throughout entire school days. It was a first. Then the slushie flavor began causing riots. One morning, it was like the storming of the Bastille, on a much smaller scale. Sadly, this left Figgins no choice but to discontinue the flavor, much to the dismay of the student body and even some teachers.

If something as small as a frozen beverage could cause riots at McKinley, the sudden onslaught of celebrity appearances was bound to get everyone riled up. All week, people had buzzed over Rachel's return, and that morning, when Santana had shown up, the kids started going ballistic. Rachel and Kurt didn't realize that by bringing in her friends from New York, they'd effectively sent a few more innocent victims into the lion's den that was McKinley High.

As soon as they entered the choir room, Meredith and Carmine were mobbed by a group of unfortunate-looking teenagers. The stars had been recognized, of course, for their work on prime-time television and in popular music, respectively. It was all going exactly according to Rachel's plan to get everyone to love her again. But her new friends were not the charming people she'd hoped for. Rachel watched the ridiculous scene from the doorway.

Meredith and Carmine were looking around at the group of adoring fans. Sure, they were small and covered with zits. Half of them were wearing really unflattering purple costumes. But Meredith regarded them as if they were a pack of zombies trying to eat her brains.

"Ew! I think that one just touched me!" she screeched, clinging on to Carmine.

What Rachel didn't remember was that Meredith Stewart

and Carmine Bennett were not used to talking to "normal" people. They were famous. They liked to surround themselves with only other people of importance or people who would tell them that *they* were important. Meredith and Carmine had only agreed to come to Ohio and perform with Rachel Berry because they were afraid of what would happen if they didn't. Rachel, as the star of *Oklahoma!*, had a lot of influence over the producers of the show. They were just her supporting costars. It was a bitter pill to swallow — especially since they had both been in the business much longer than Rachel had. But they knew how to keep their friends close and their enemies closer.

Rachel crossed over into the room. She was about to ask her guests if they needed anything when she was startled by Meredith's shrill voice.

"Get away from me, you teenaged freak!" Meredith screamed at the red-haired boy — the only one who had been brave enough to ask Meredith to take a picture with him. Meredith wrapped her arms tightly around her body, disgusted. The poor boy, looking extremely hurt, walked back to his friends.

Carmine wasn't much better. A tiny girl with glasses and a blond ponytail had come up to him and shyly confessed that the very first concert she'd ever been to was one of his.

"Is that supposed to impress me?" he replied snottily. He looked to Meredith for backup that this girl was, indeed, an idiot. Meredith laughed.

Well, they just lost a few fans, Rachel thought as she

watched in disbelief. She couldn't imagine ever being that harsh to anyone, let alone fans.

And then she remembered her nickname, Scary Berry. All of a sudden, she felt like she'd been hit with a ton of bricks. What if she *was* actually this horrible to people now, too? Everyone had been implying it nonstop since she'd landed here. Coach Sylvester had said Rachel didn't care whom she hurt to get what she wanted. Kurt had said she was selfish. Meredith and Carmine were supposedly her best friends now.

It all added up. Rachel had become a horrible person.

She felt sick. She had wanted fame but not like this. She wanted to be adored, but for who she was and her talents. She wanted to be Glinda the Good Witch, not the Wicked Witch of the West (even if she was just a misunderstood green girl played by Idina Menzel in one of the best new Broadway shows in recent memory). Rachel had to do something to change her life.

The crowd rumbled and roared outside, chanting for the rally to start. Meredith and Carmine looked at Rachel expectantly.

Rachel took a deep breath and steeled herself for her entrance. The show must go on. Even if it meant performing with a couple of evil flying monkeys.

sixteen

McKinley High gymnasium, end-of-year rally,
Thursday afternoon

"Oh my God," Rachel said as she peeked out from behind the black curtain that had been set up as a backstage area. Her eyes widened. "There must be over two thousand people out there!"

She had never seen the gym this packed in her entire time at McKinley. There were several professional television camera crews up front and even a few amateur ones. Students spilled over onto the sides of the court, creating a makeshift amphitheater. Red and white streamers exploded from the ceiling like a gigantic chandelier, and bunches of balloons were tied to the backs of the bleachers.

The chants of the crowd echoed off the walls and grew louder with each passing moment. "Mc-Kin-ley! Mc-Kin-ley! Mc-Kin-ley!" they shouted. It looked like a scene out of a sports movie, and it was weird because the community had never gotten this excited about any team at the school. It was almost like the gym was being used properly for the first time.

Rachel closed her eyes and took it all in. There was an amazing energy in the room, and she wanted to remember it forever. Especially since this would probably be her last time in this gym. The thought of it put a lump in her throat. She began to hum it out. *Hummmm.*

The crowd roared as the Cheerios ran out onto the court, clad in their trademark red-and-black uniforms. Rachel turned around to look at Brittany. She was curious to see if Brittany was wishing she were out on the court with her old squad. If she was, her face didn't show it. She just stood there in her starfish costume, a massive smile plastered on her face like she was having the best time in the world. She probably was. Brittany could be happy in almost any situation. It was an admirable quality.

Back on the court, Mercedes had picked up the microphone and started pumping up the crowd even more. *"Are... You... Ready?"* Mercedes yelled over the screams and shouts. "I *said* — Are! You! Red! E?" Even the moms were getting into it now. It was almost starting to look like the audience of an "Oprah's Favorite Things" episode, where people practically threw one another across the room every time they were gifted something from the list.

Rachel could see Mercedes's mom in the crowd. She was

yelling at the top of her lungs, "That's my baby! That's my girl!" Rachel thought it was sweet how proud of Mercedes she was. And she should have been. The way Mercedes was working the crowd was amazing. She was a natural born leader, commanding the entire room with ease.

Finally, Mercedes took her spot in formation. The crowd hushed for a moment.

The speakers began to blast a beat, and the Cheerios sprang into action. Mercedes spun around, dancing the routine like she'd choreographed it herself. From what Rachel had heard, she probably had. The song morphed into "Dynamite," by Taio Cruz. Mercedes began to belt it out, and the squad moved in perfect time behind her. Rachel found herself dancing and clapping her hands in time to the beat along with everyone else.

By the time the routine ended a few minutes later, Rachel was feeling really pumped up. So was the entire gym. The Cheerios had always been incredible, but under Mercedes's reign, they had rocketed themselves to unreal status. It made Rachel wonder what other innovative routines she hadn't gotten to see at various events throughout the school year. If they had been anything like this one had been, she'd seriously missed out. Maybe she had underestimated Mercedes back in their Glee days. Rachel knew it was too late for regrets, but if she could go back, she would let Mercedes have a lot more solos. The girl deserved them.

But apparently, Mercedes knew that. The success as head

Cheerio had gone straight to her head. As she exited the court, a nerdy freshman girl came up to Mercedes. Rachel knew the type — desperate to join the Cheerios, to be popular, but not quite talented or pretty enough to get in. It was like watching a silent movie from across the gym. Mercedes totally snubbed the girl and went off to go sit with her uniform-clad posse. The cycle was complete. Mercedes used to be so nice. It was a shame to have lost her to the dark depths of high school popularity.

Even over the loud rumble of the crowd, Meredith's distinctive cackle rang out. Rachel had completely forgotten that Meredith and Carmine were with her.

Meredith chewed on a piece of her ginger-colored hair and stared lovingly at Carmine, who continued to tap away at the touch screen on his phone.

"So, are you guys having fun?" Rachel asked, knowing full well that they were miserable.

"This is like watching *Grease*," Carmine said.

It was a much nicer comment than Rachel had expected. "Oh, yeah?"

"Yeah. There's horrible dancing, and the music makes my ears bleed," he responded in a deadpan voice. Meredith laughed. She was either easily amused or totally crushing. The comment wasn't even that funny.

The New New Directions were up next. Brittany led her band of purple-clad starfish out onto the floor. There was a little cheering from the audience and a lot of confused whispers.

"Should we bother with this one, Paul?" a WOHN television guy asked his coworker quite loudly.

"No," Paul answered.

Once everyone was in position, Brittany freed the microphone from the stand. "Hey, everyone," she said in her quiet voice. It was a stark contrast to Mercedes's booming tone. "This song is dedicated to all the endangered starfish in the glitter region of the rainbow sea. It's a bad situation down there right now, people. Don't be blind." The entire gym had fallen silent out of pure confusion rather than respect. "Thank you." Brittany took her place.

After a weird yet peppy rendition of "Baby, I'm a Star" by Prince — in which *star* had been cleverly changed to *starfish* — the Glee Club kids ran off the stage, dodging empty cups and jeers from the large audience. Seemed like it was still hard to be a Glee kid. At least they looked like they were having fun. Rachel remembered banding together with her club in solidarity, too. It was nice.

"What is this — amateur hour?" Meredith whined loudly before making a big show of employing a pair of neon-green earplugs. "My ears are too precious to listen to any more of this garbage."

The residual good feelings from watching the show vanished as Rachel realized it was almost time to go out there herself. Her feet throbbed in pain as she began to pace in a circle. She was nervous. Really nervous. This was her hometown. These were her peers. Who could be harsher judges than them? It was still a mystery to Rachel why she'd decided to come back here in the first place. But then again, a lot of things about her new life were mysterious.

Rachel, Meredith, and Carmine were supposed to go on next. After Figgins announced them and the crowd had a few moments to go wild, she would go out there and sing her heart out. And then everything would be fine. All of Lima would see that Rachel Berry *did* actually possess genuine talent, as well as humility. She had not forgotten where she'd come from, even if she'd left it for greener pastures. Or taller skyscrapers.

But when Rachel looked up, Figgins wasn't standing on the court at all. *Finn* was.

He tapped on the microphone gently a few times before bringing it to his mouth. This caused it to peak, and the whole speaker system screeched for a terrible second.

"Sorry. Oh, um, hey, everybody! Uhh...so...I just wanted to know if I could have just a moment of your attention before continuing on with the show." He shifted back and forth on his feet.

What was he doing? Rachel thought. Was he going to... break out in song?

Finn removed the microphone from its stand. "So. There's a really special girl here today...."

Rachel held her breath. Finn was going to declare his love for her! In front of everyone. She took a small step forward. Maybe everything was going to be all right, after all. Finn could get his tattoo removed and come with her to New York, and they would live happily—

"Her name is Quinn Fabray."

Rachel's stomach dropped.

Everyone else began to cheer. Quinn stood up from where she was sitting on the floor and sheepishly waved at the crowd. Her blond curls glowed in the yellow-tinted light.

"Now...I'm not a man of many words. So, uh...I'll just get down to it." Finn reached for something in his pocket. "I love you, Quinn Fabray." He kneeled. "Will you marry me?" He held out a little velvet box. Rachel could see the inside of it sparkling all the way across the gym.

The crowd held its breath in anticipation.

After what seemed like an eternity—but was probably only really about five seconds—Quinn skipped over to Finn and gave him a huge kiss. He then scooped her up into his arms and spun her around in a circle. He held the microphone up to her mouth.

She giggled as she clarified, "Yes. I said yes." Finn made a big show of sliding the ring onto her finger. It was all tragically unoriginal.

The applause was deafening as Finn carried Quinn off the court, bride-style. Rachel couldn't bring herself to clap or anything. It was too painful. She was secretly embarrassed for thinking Finn might have decided he loved her instead. The thought alone made her cheeks hot.

Like Meredith had said earlier, it was time to get on with the show and get out. The past five minutes had been a game changer, and Rachel just wanted to bolt.

Principal Figgins treaded out to the center of the floor.

He fumbled with the microphone and dropped it on the ground.

"What an exciting day!" he finally announced in the robotic voice he reserved especially for public speaking. "Okay, okay. Settle down. As you know, I'm Principal Figgins. I am the principal here at William McKinley High School. We have had a great school year and hope to have many more to come." He cleared his throat loudly. It sounded phlegmy. "Now it is my pleasure to introduce a special guest—McKinley's own Rachel Berry!" There was a sparse round of applause and a few cheers. "Joining her are her costars from Broadway, Miss Meredith Stewart and Mr. Carmen, excuse me—*Carmine* Bennett!" His name elicited squeals of girly delight from the Cheerios section.

Rachel stepped out in front of the gigantic crowd. It was surreal. It was the audience she'd always envisioned performing for when she'd gone to school here. Hundreds of people cheering, just waiting to hear her belt out a song of her choosing at the top of her lungs. Rachel used to joke with Finn that she needed applause to live. Maybe it was true. She felt slightly rejuvenated in the face of the crowd.

She looked to her left and right, fully expecting to see Meredith and Carmine beside her. But she was alone. This was beginning to become a theme.

A few moments later, the tardy twins scampered out onto the court. They instantly transformed from the horrible, whiny brats they were into glittering stars. Their smiles directed at the sea of people and cameras seemed completely genuine. Hundreds of cameras flashed in their direction. Meredith was working it. Rachel tried to remember the angles Kurt had taught her. *Kurt.* She felt a pang in her gut at the thought of him.

Now was not the time, though.

"It's so great to be back here at McKinley," Rachel said into the microphone. "I never realized how much I missed you all until I came back." It was really true. Seeing everyone and how they'd changed had started to make her realize just what she'd missed while she was living in New York. "This one is for my all my old friends from New Directions."

She looked to Carmine and Meredith, hoping that Kurt had filled them in on the song change. Rachel didn't really think a medley of songs from *Oklahoma!* fit the occasion, so the switch was decided that morning. She'd chosen "In My Life" by the Beatles. It was a classic. And she was a classy girl.

Carmine nodded at her, and the soft piano music began.

Rachel sang the first verse. *"There are places I remember all my life, though some have changed."* The Beatles' lyrics were eerily appropriate for her current state of mind, even though she'd chosen them earlier.

As she sang, Rachel scanned the audience for familiar faces. There were some that she recognized from having classes together or seeing in the hallways. Others were just kids who had once thrown slushies in her face. She recognized a few of the parents from events or chaperoning dances. It made her sad that the adults in her life were not present. She missed her dads. And she even missed goofy Mr. Schuester.

Rachel joined in with the lead vocals as Meredith and Carmine began to sing a gorgeous harmony. A janitor near the door listened and began to sway with his mop.

For some reason, Rachel couldn't take her eyes off that janitor. He was so into the music. He looked an awful lot like...No. It couldn't be. Sometimes staring out into a crowd played tricks on a person. It was easy to imagine seeing someone you wished was there.

The song ended, and Rachel took a bow.

seventeen

McKinley High hallway, after the performance,
Thursday afternoon

After she was finished with her own song, Rachel
didn't feel it necessary to stick around and watch
Santana's scandalous pop performance. It was
bound to be a spectacle, but Rachel just wasn't in the mood.
She'd watched as Santana had sashayed out onto the basketball court wearing an outfit that was basically nothing but a
glorified bikini and cowboy boots. And judging by the
cheers and hollers that were now exploding from the gym,
she was probably shaking everything she had to a song that
was originally written for Ke$ha. No, thanks.

The beautiful song Rachel had just performed had put her
in a sentimental mood. She even felt a little like crying.
Rachel decided to go for a stroll around her favorite places at
McKinley High one more time. It would be the perfect end to

the "Rachel Berry Nostalgia Tour," as Kurt had been calling their trip to Lima all week. Rachel traced her fingers along the wall as she walked along, as if she were trying to record the memory of the place with her touch.

A little farther down the hall was the same janitor who had been digging on her song just a few minutes ago. It looked like he was grooving on something else now. Either in his mind or playing on an iPod—Rachel couldn't tell which. His feet danced around as he gave his best effort to mop the grungy linoleum. It was a lost cause, though. The floor at McKinley never looked clean because of the constant slushie and raw egg attacks on those kids unfortunate enough to be at the bottom of the social ladder, or anyone who pissed off Dave Karofksy. Dirt stuck to egg whites like nobody's business.

"Hey!" Rachel called down at him, not even sure what she wanted to ask. She had this crazy urge to talk to him. "Hey! Wait!"

The janitor glanced up at her, quickly put his head down, and tried to push his mop elsewhere. He wasn't very fast. All it took were a couple of skips, and she was right next to him.

Rachel laid her hand on the man's shoulder. "Were you just dancing back there?" she asked as he turned around to face her. Her jaw dropped. She hadn't been imagining things during her performance at all. The janitor was Mr. Schuester!

But it was no wonder that people didn't recognize him.

He looked like a shadow of his former bubbly, Journey-singing self. His eyes were sunken in like he hadn't slept in days, and his unruly curly hair had grown out and looked like an overgrown weed. It was as if Sue Sylvester's nightmare had come to life.

"Mr. Schuester? Is that really you?" Rachel asked, grateful to finally have found the missing piece of the puzzle.

He nodded sadly. But Rachel didn't understand why he was mopping floors in a jumpsuit instead of parading around the halls in a vest and talking about feelings.

"What's happened to you?" What was this, *Good Will Schuester*?

"It's a long story, Rachel. I don't know if I want to go into it...." He plopped the mop back in his bucket. Water splashed out and nearly ruined Rachel's shoes. She jumped back a few inches. "Your voice sounded beautiful in there. I'm very happy for you." He sounded like he was truly happy for her. But he was still very depressed for himself.

"Aw, come on Mr. Schu," she begged. Rachel knew he'd always had a rough personal life. His divorce had broken his heart once—and then Miss Pillsbury, the guidance counselor, had broken it again right after that by marrying her dentist, Carl Howell. Maybe the hard times he'd fallen on had something to do with that. Love is rough. "Was it Miss Pillsbury?"

"No, no." He gazed straight into Rachel's eyes. "If it had to do with anyone, I'd say it was actually you."

Oh no. Rachel didn't want what Puck had implied about her and Mr. Schuester to be true. That would be so weird and inappropriate. She shuddered at the thought of it.

"Nothing romantic, of course," he added, reading the terrified expression on her face. He didn't need to remind her of the Suzy Pepper moment. But Rachel's crush on Mr. Schuester hadn't bordered on obsession, like Suzy's had.

"No, I never thought that for a second. Not even a little bit. Why would you say that?" Rachel's words spilled out faster than she'd intended.

"Just a hunch," Mr. Schuester said as he poured some more blue solution labeled KLEEN RITE into his vat of dirty mop water. It looked the same. Rachel seriously doubted that it was going to do anything more than spread the dirt and germs around more evenly.

"So are you going to tell me what really happened?" Rachel asked. "Or do I have to make you sing about it?" So Will Schuester liked to sing out his troubles—big deal. A lot of other people did it, too. Like B.B. King and Ray Charles. It was called the blues.

"I'm sure you have figured this out by now, but a lot changed when you left, Rachel." The way he leaned on his mop looked like he was about to start waltzing with it at any second.

Rachel tried not to take this information as a compliment, but it was hard not to. It meant that she mattered.

"After you landed that Broadway role and Santana got 'discovered' by that record producer in such quick succession, people started to notice. They thought the common thread was me and my brilliant teaching skills. My students were hitting it big left and right!" A smile danced on his lips and threatened to form, but never fully did. "So when you and Sue came to me about starting my own vocal training academy in New York...I jumped at the chance." He looked off into the distance. "I've always loved singing. Why wouldn't I want to give it a try in New York at least once?"

"So I was the one who persuaded you to leave McKinley and New Directions?" Rachel wasn't pleased with the news that she was to blame for all this. It just made her feel lower than she did already—which was pretty low. Mr. Schuester began to push the mop bucket as he walked down the hall. Rachel followed, eager to hear more.

"Well, you and Sue together. You don't remember?" He furrowed his brow, like he was worried that he was the one who'd started forgetting details about his life.

Rachel shook her head. "Refresh me."

But Mr. Schuester looked like he was holding something back. "Well, I used all my savings to rent a studio in New York that I could live in and run voice classes out of. It was great for a while."

Rachel hung on to his every word. She'd completely forgotten that the rally was about to let out.

They strolled for a little while in silence as Mr. Schuester gathered his thoughts. He stopped at a brown door marked MAINTENANCE. How funny. It was the exact same janitor's closet Rachel was going to go do her warm-ups in earlier.

"Then what?" Rachel prodded.

He shot her a look that warned her not to push it. "One of the main selling points of my new academy was your endorsement. Not only did you refuse to give it, but you publicly denied having ever known me! You said that everything you knew you had taught yourself." Mr. Schuester shook his head in pity. "It *ruined* me, Rachel. Everyone called me a fraud. No one would come to the academy anymore! I lost my studio. I lost everything." He got out his gigantic ring of keys and unlocked the door. "Luckily, a kind stranger took pity on me and let me hitch a ride back to Lima. But I've basically been trying to pull myself out of the gutter ever since." He sat down in an old, decomposing armchair. The acid-green color helped slightly in hiding the mold spots.

Rachel didn't think she could feel any worse. But then she saw the blankets rumpled up in the corner. "Mr. Schu — are you *living* here?" She was going to fix this. Mr. Schuester living in a janitor's closet at McKinley High was totally unacceptable. He was her mentor, not a homeless janitor.

Suddenly, Rachel flashed back to Monday night. She'd been leaving the mini-mart when a curly-haired man had startled her, saying he knew her. Rachel had accidentally slushied him! The man was Mr. Schuester! She looked down at him in his dirty chair and tan jumpsuit. The blue patch on his chest said WILL.

"Principal Figgins said I could pick up some janitorial work on the side until I get on my feet again. There has been a problem lately with kids 'buttering' the floors, and they needed extra mopping help. Luckily they'd kept my uniform." Mr. Schuester had worked briefly as a McKinley night janitor during Rachel's sophomore year. He was just trying to earn extra cash then. Nothing like this. "Originally, he was going to let me run Glee Club. But, of course, there was no money in the budget to hire a teacher solely for that purpose. And the district wouldn't allow a janitor to run it." He smiled and let out a chuckle. "But with some luck, Figgins said he might be able to hire me to teach Spanish again next school year. So that's good."

Rachel couldn't believe Mr. Schuester's ability to remain positive in a situation like this.

"Mr. Schu, I can't let you live like this. Especially if it's my fault!" She bit her lip. "Please let me help you out."

He threw his hands up in protest. "I think I've had enough of your 'help,' Rachel."

People began to trickle out of the gym. Soon, the hallways would be packed. Rachel needed to duck and cover before she got mobbed.

"I have to run. But please reconsider my offer. I'm so sorry, Mr. Schu." And she really was.

Rachel ran to the choir room as fast as her stilettos would take her. Too bad they couldn't take her back in time.

eighteen

Lima Youth Center, Thursday afternoon

The afternoon's conversation with Mr. Schuester had left Rachel feeling like an absolutely deplorable person. It had been heart-wrenching to listen to his woes. He had been so unlucky, and she felt partially responsible for leading him down the garden path. Not that she remembered doing any of those things. But still, he had blamed her for his misfortune and then added insult to injury by not letting her make it right. She wanted to help him in his time of need. Mr. Schuester had done so much for her throughout the years. He'd done so much for everyone. There had to be a way to even the scales again.

Rachel had returned to the choir room to gather some of her things right after seeing him. It was almost empty now except for a few stragglers — kids taking off the rest of their elaborate starfish costumes.

Rachel's monogrammed duffel bag with the gold stars on it sat right where she had left it in the corner. Rachel was thankful she had listened to Kurt about bringing a change of comfortable clothes with her. These glamorous ones didn't feel like her at all anymore. Her feet ached, and she was tired of pulling down the back of her skirt when it rode up into scandalous territory. She just wanted to be plain old Rachel Berry again. Why was it, again, that she had never been happy with herself before? It was hard to remember.

The clock on the wall read 3:30. Almost time to fly back to New York and spend every waking minute with those two pains known as Carmine Bennett and Meredith Stewart. Celebrity friends were not as cool as she'd thought they'd be.

Rachel wondered where they had gone. They'd probably dashed the second their song was over and caught the first flight back to the city. But Rachel couldn't really judge — she'd ditched everyone, too.

She went behind her little sports blanket curtain and changed into the blue jeans and red tank top from her bag — and, of course, her favorite glittery red ballet flats. She must have had those things forever. They weren't even expensive. She slid a thin white headband into her hair. That was better. It was like when Superman turned back into Clark Kent. He probably welcomed that nerdy suit and glasses after the stress of wearing spandex in front of huge crowds. Talk about pressure.

It was hard to decide her next move. She'd lost Kurt — and he was the one who had all the answers. He'd done a great job of keeping her schedule and keeping her well dressed. She shouldn't have been so harsh with him about the pictures. There were worse things in life than a leaked personal picture on a fan site dedicated to your hotness. Mr. Schuester was evidence of that.

Several pairs of footsteps grew louder in the hallway. Laughter accompanied them. Rachel went to the door to see who was having so much fun. Rachel's heart fluttered as she saw a beautiful thing — it was Kurt leading a pack of her old Glee friends! Brittany and Santana were there (doing that hand-holding thing they liked to do), followed by Quinn, Finn, and Puck. Several of the new Glee kids whom Rachel didn't know took up the rear.

Rachel ran out in front of them. "Hey, guys! Where are you going?" The scene felt totally normal. She was comfortable as an attention-hungry geek. The setting brought it out in her. Kurt looked her up and down, assessing the full transformation back to Glee Club Rachel.

"If I hadn't heard your song and dedication at the rally, I wouldn't bother telling you," Kurt said. "I'd think you wouldn't want to come anyway. But you do appear to have a shred of a soul left."

Happiness radiated from Finn and Quinn — who kept gazing down at her ring finger when she thought no one was looking.

"We're going to the Lima Youth Center to sing with the

kids. We go every Thursday," Quinn said. She cocked her head. "Do you want to come?"

Finn smiled hopefully.

Did they really want her to go with them? Rachel wondered. It sounded kind of fun. And perhaps she could earn back some of that good karma she was so seriously lacking.

Santana chimed in. "I called some photographers. It will totes make it into *Superstar Weekly*, if you are on the fence." Santana was so predictable. "I mean, they're no PS 22 Choir," she said, referring to the famous elementary school choir from Staten Island in New York. "But they aren't bad. They're cute kids."

"It sounds great," Rachel said, and actually meant it.

Rachel went with them to the youth center, and she was so glad she did. Santana was right—the kids were fantastic singers. Rachel could hardly believe how much fun it was to listen to them sing and give them pointers. They were so motivated, too. Almost like tiny versions of herself! Her favorite was a little Japanese girl named Kiku—she had one of the prettiest voices she'd ever heard on a third grader who wasn't even eight years old.

At the end of their time together, the kids chose a song for everyone to sing together. Kiku's older sister had put the song "Change" by Taylor Swift on her iPod, and Kiku was absolutely desperate for them to sing it. Kurt obliged, saying that Taylor Swift was one of his contemporary idols—her spunky country attitude and spot-on fashion sense made him feel like they were meant to be best friends and shopping partners. He set about giving each person parts to sing.

After a few practice runs, the group went full out. Their voices joined together to make such a rich sound, and Rachel was in awe that kids so young could pick up on something so fast. It made her feel like an idiot for being so closed-minded last summer about Mr. Schuester's music camp. If it had been anything like today, it would have been more than enough to make her summer great. *Oh, well*, Rachel thought as they all said good-bye to the kids. *What's done is done.*

By the time Rachel and Kurt were finished saying good-bye to all the New Directions alumni, it was getting really late.

"We have to hurry if we want to get back to New York tonight," Kurt reminded Rachel. They quickly headed back to the school to pick up their stuff, which they'd left in the choir room.

Rachel and Kurt sprinted through the hallways to the choir room. It felt just like *The Breakfast Club*. They had really cut things much too short, time-wise. The two of them huffed and puffed. But it was funny.

Through deep breaths and laughter, Kurt yelled out, "Rachel...I'm...sorry!" He stopped and put his hands on his knees to catch his breath. He was surprisingly out of shape. "I'm sorry...about the pictures. I shouldn't have done that," he squeaked as they began to jog. They were almost there.

"No...*I* am. I understand...why you did it!" Rachel

yelled back, laughing. They both stopped and looked at each other.

"Friends?" Rachel said.

"Friends," Kurt answered.

They laughed together. Rachel was glad that was finally resolved! She leaned in for a hug, but something was really slippery. Rachel struggled to keep her balance but couldn't because the floor was covered in butter! It was a classic McKinley High School prank that was normally reserved for substitute teachers. Janitor Schuester had missed a spot. Rachel slipped, falling right into Kurt. *Smack!*

Their heads knocked together. Hard.

And the last thing Rachel saw before passing out was one of her glittery ruby slippers flying through the air....

nineteen

Rachel's bedroom, present day, Monday night

achel tried to blink open her eyes, but the throbbing in her head made it almost impossible. *Ouch.* She attempted to sit up. Rachel gingerly rubbed the large bump that was now beginning to form on her forehead. How long had she been out for? She scanned her bedroom for a clock but didn't see one immediately.

She and Kurt must have hit their heads *really* hard if someone was able to bring her all the way back home without waking her up. Wait a second — home? Her bedroom? Rachel looked around again, as if it were all going to crumble to dust at any second. Did she miss the jet? Where was the jet?

She blinked hard, finally sitting up. Her eyes landed on her *Wicked* calendar on the wall. That was her calendar from last year! The little green x's she'd made as a countdown to the end of the school year seemed to say there was still a little less than a week left to go. Her brand-new Patti Lupone ceramic bust lay broken on the ground next to where she was sitting. And all around her, glittery tissue paper littered the floor.

Panic overtook her as Rachel suddenly realized that she couldn't feel her toes. Upon closer inspection, it looked as if they had lost all circulation because of some ridiculously painful shoes she had on. Thank goodness for that. She ripped each shoe off violently and threw them across the room. She wiggled her toes, and the tingly feeling began to dissipate. *Ahhh, that's better.*

Da-dum! Da-dum! A strange noise came from somewhere. What was that? It sounded really familiar, but Rachel couldn't seem to make sense of anything. It all looked so fuzzy....*Da-dum!* There it was again. She looked around. It sounded like...an instant message?

Rachel stood up and ran over to her computer. Sure enough, a chat window blinked like a strobe light. Several messages awaited her from someone with the screen name Sharkfinn5. It was Finn! *Rach, I'm really sorry about the way things went at dinner tonight,* Finn wrote. *If you want to go to dance class and stuff, I'm cool with it. You don't have to do the dumb camp thing with all of us.* Then he'd obviously gotten worried when she hadn't responded. *You there? Rach? Rachel? Are you still mad at me?*

So...she was in her bedroom in Lima. The calendar on the wall was from last year. And Finn was talking to her!

Finally, Rachel was lifted out of her haze. All of a sudden, she came to the stunning realization that it had been an extremely long, horrible, stressful dream. *Whoa. More like a nightmare, actually.* But it was all over!

Sure it'd had its winning moments — like the private jet — but Rachel Berry had never been so happy to be in her own bedroom again. This was the best she'd felt in forever, even with a head injury. She knew exactly what to do now, and she felt so lucky that she still had a chance to make things right. Rachel didn't want to miss a single thing this summer or next year in Glee Club. Fame and fortune could wait. At least for a little bit.

Finn's chat window still flashed, violently demanding a response.

I'm back! she wrote. *And you were right — the camp sounds like a blast. I can't wait to hang out with you guys and a bunch of kids all summer. Career can wait for once.*

She heard the door slam downstairs.

"Rachel! We're home!" her dad Hiram yelled up the stairs.

"We bought sorbet! Come down and have some!" her dad Leroy added.

"Be there in a second!" she hollered back, brimming with anticipation to run down and see them and never let them go. She just had one more thing to do. She clicked on the document titled RACHEL'S STAR POWER SUMMER! and hit the DELETE button without a single shred of hesitation.

Then Rachel ran downstairs. She had an appointment to have dessert with her two biggest fans.

twenty

Choir room, Tuesday morning

There he was. Standing by the piano, wearing a navy pinstripe vest and looking over some stacks of sheet music. Rachel couldn't express how relieved and happy she felt when she saw Mr. Schuester back at his normal post, looking the same as he always had. His curly hair was combed (though Coach Sylvester would claim otherwise), and he was tapping his foot to some invisible song in his head. He was probably planning a new song for them to sing at the rally. Mr. Schuester never gave up on trying to find the best music for them. Rachel could tell how much he loved and appreciated each member of New Directions.

And Rachel appreciated him, too.

"Mr. Schuester!" Rachel barged into the room, a wide, cheesy smile plastered on her face.

Mr. Schuester raised his left eyebrow suspiciously. Usually that look meant that Rachel had some crazy idea that he was going to have to find a nice way to shoot down.

"Yes, Rachel?"

"I just wanted to tell you to rip up that schedule I gave you. You won't be needing it anymore."

Mr. Schuester rolled his eyes. "Why? . . . Are you giving me a revised copy?"

Rachel shook her head. "I've decided to join everyone as camp director for the McKinley High Summer Youth Music Camp!"

Mr. Schuester was genuinely impressed. Rachel Berry never canceled her plans for anything or anyone. Unless it was Andrew Lloyd Webber. She would *definitely* cancel something for him.

"That's fantastic, Rachel! The kids are going to be happy to have you! And so are we." Mr. Schuester gave her a hug. "I'm really proud of you."

"I'm proud of me, too," she said with a wink, and took her seat.

Ten minutes later, everyone sat around and listened as Rachel told them the news. They were all really excited, until Rachel began to list her massive agenda as camp director — a position to which she hadn't even been elected yet.

"Well, I have this idea for a number involving starfish costumes. . . ."

"Sounds awesome," Brittany whispered, looking much more normal now that she was in her Cheerios uniform.

Mr. Schuester butted in. "Guys, we have plenty of time to plan and discuss this later. But now, let's go show those future campers what New Directions is made of!"

After they'd performed a rockin' rendition of Miley Cyrus's "Party In The U.S.A." for a packed gym and an adorable group of elementary school kids, Rachel was feeling pretty fantastic. She had a summer full of fun and singing with her friends ahead of her, and an entire year to go before she had to get serious about her career. Life was pretty good. Just when she thought things couldn't get any better, a little red-haired girl in a purple dress ran up to her.

"You sing *really* pretty!" she said, eyes wide with admiration. Rachel bent down and took the little girl's hand.

"Aw, thank you so much! What's your name?"

The little girl smiled. "I'm Megan. Megan Smithson."

Rachel smiled devilishly and put a hand on Megan's shoulder. "Megan, how would you like me, Rachel Berry, to give you private singing lessons?"

OFFICIAL *GLEE* NOVELS:

MORE REFRESHING THAN A SLUSHIE IN THE FACE...

AVAILABLE NOW

www.ReadGlee.com

BOB383

Where stories bloom.

poppy

Visit us online at
www.pickapoppy.com